"Long time, no see." His mouth twisted determinedly. *"Surprise, darlin'!"*

Nathan!

The prickle of t  ed into an outbreak of swe alyzed, she could only sta y eyes. She stiffened aga prayer barely squeaked pa

Nathan stepped forward and she began to jerk back, but her feet remained firmly planted. She couldn't even let go of the bags clenched so tightly in her hands.

"What?" his deep voice taunted cruelly. "You don't recognize your own husband?"

Judi went cold. What she wouldn't do for a trapdoor to swallow her whole. Matter of fact, this would be a fine time to check out of the horrendous situation with an elaborate fainting spell like the heroines in those sappy novels, yet she knew even the most contrived luxury of unconsciousness would never happen for her. No, life would force her to be cognizant of every miserable second.

Unprepared! She felt utterly unprepared. After months of readiness, her preparation for such a moment had been stymied by the calm she'd experienced on the island. His impeccable shirt and tie routine didn't help matters. He always dressed the part when he meant business, and right now the solemn expression on his face indicated every last fiber of his being was dead serious.

Biting back the fear, Judi cast Nathan an anxious glance. "What are you doing here?" she blurted.

He looked stunned at her question and laughed—a heartless, unamused laugh. Then his jaw squared and his eyes turned into chipped ice. "You're unbelievable! I come to Bay Island to find my supposedly dead wife and all you can say is 'What are you doing here?'"

BETH LOUGHNER has worked several years as a regular columnist and has written for various magazines and three full-length dramas. She began writing in 1990 while enjoying her years as a stay-at-home mom. Beth also finds great excitement in her occupation as a registered nurse.

Through her writing, she hopes to inspire others to find the true character of God and to encourage readers to apply these truths to their lives. Her husband and two children have made the beautiful state of Ohio their home. They love traveling to unusual places within the state and beyond its borders. Visit Beth's Web site at www.bethloughner.com.

Books by Beth Loughner

HEARTSONG PRESENTS
HP553—Bay Island
HP685—Thunder Bay

Bay
Hideaway

Beth Loughner

Heartsong Presents

Special thanks to Becky Rickard for all of her editing services. I couldn't have done it without you.

Deep appreciation goes to Bill Hedrick, city of Columbus prosecuting attorney, for his legal expertise.

A big thank-you to Pennsylvania State Representative Karen Beyer and her assistant, Maurine Payne, for sharing their knowledge of the Pennsylvania Statehouse.

A note from the Author:
I love to hear from my readers! You may correspond with me by writing:

Beth Loughner
Author Relations
PO Box 721
Uhrichsville, OH 44683

ISBN 978-1-59789-386-2

BAY HIDEAWAY

All scriptures are taken from the King James Version of the Bible.

All of the characters and events in this book are fictitious. Any resemblance to actual persons, living or dead, or to actual events is purely coincidental.

Our mission is to publish and distribute inspirational products offering exceptional value and biblical encouragement to the masses.

PRINTED IN THE U.S.A.

prologue

Are you absolutely positive?" Nathaniel Whithorne gripped the desk with one hand and sank slowly into his expensive desk chair.

"It's her!" the male voice at the other end of the line answered. "It's your wife."

The leather creaked softly as Nathaniel swiveled the chair toward the floor-to-ceiling plates of glass overlooking the city of Harrisburg, Pennsylvania. The bright sun bounced off an adjacent building, reflecting shards of light into his office. For a moment he was speechless. What could he say? He let the back of his knuckles slide back and forth against the square of his clean-shaven jaw. How could he believe the unbelievable in spite of his suspicions?

"Representative Whithorne?" the voice continued. "Are you still there?"

The spray of light coming through the windows slowly seeped out of the room, and Nathaniel's reflection in the glass began to take form. He stared back. His thick black hair was now peppered with gray—a change his regal mother would say enhanced his already aristocratic features. But his features were more haggard than ever and he knew it. He'd aged more over the past two years than during his entire forty.

Suddenly, he swung the chair back toward the massive mahogany desk. "Where is she?"

"On a small Ohio island off Lake Erie," answered the man. "It's called Bay Island—a touristy type place for summer travelers."

"And you're sure it's Judi?"

"I've seen her, sir!" the man assured confidently. "There's no mistake. She's going by the name of Amanda Judith Rydell, but the islanders call her Judi. There are photos I can send you."

"Where's she living on the island?"

"North Shore Condominiums." The sound of shuffling papers came across the line. "The actual address is 791 Wind Surf Drive, Unit E."

Nathan penned the address onto an ivory writing pad. "And her work?"

"Working as a church secretary, sir."

"Church secretary?" Surprise riddled Nathan's voice.

"Yes, sir!"

"Book me a place to stay and ground transportation for this Bay Island place," ordered Nathan. "I'm leaving tomorrow morning."

"But, sir—"

"Use your name for the reservations," Nathan went on uninterrupted. "Under no circumstances do I want her knowing about my arrival." He paused a moment. "And, Thomas?"

"Yes, sir?"

"I don't think I need to tell you how important it is for you to keep this information under wraps. Do you understand? No leaks."

"Yes, sir!"

"You'll need to cancel my appointments for the next few days." Nathan flipped open his daily planner. "Make my apologies and reschedule what you can."

"What about House Bill 65?" questioned Thomas. "It's due for a vote on Thursday."

Nathan groaned. "See what you can do to stall the vote. I can't miss that bill when it hits the floor."

"Yes, sir."

"And, Thomas?"

"Yes, sir?"

"You don't have to keep addressing me as *sir* in private."

"I know, sir."

Nathan gave a sigh of resignation. "One last thing—hand deliver all the original photos and information you have. Don't make copies."

"Yes, sir."

"Thanks for covering this, Thomas."

"My pleasure, sir. Will there be anything else?"

Nathan tapped his pen on the desk as he thought a moment. "No. If you get my transportation and reservations in order, I'll take it from there." He leaned back in the chair. "I'll call you as soon as I know how much time I'm going to need. It's not a small matter when it comes to raising the dead."

"Sounds gruesome, sir."

"I'm sure it will be!"

one

Judi Rydell casually looked up from the computer screen as the church office door swooshed open. Her fingers stilled, hovering lightly over the keyboard, her finely manicured nails making light contact with the keys.

"Good morning," called the blond visitor with obvious enthusiasm, his tall figure striding purposefully through the doorway and straight to the waist-high, natural oak counter. His smiling, raven-haired wife followed.

"You're both early," Judi commented with a slight smile. "What's the occasion?" She watched in amusement as the man's gaze darted sharply toward the clock above her.

A playful smirk crossed Larry Newkirk's lips. "It's Wednesday and ten o'clock. What more do you want?"

"Nine fifty-nine if you want to be exact."

He consulted his gold wristwatch. "According to my precision-made Swiss timepiece, it's ten to be exact—and hence, a moot point." His mischievous eyes dared her to contradict, and when she only shrugged, he continued. "Got anything for us?"

Judi pushed her chair back and lightly stretched as she stood. "Actually, I do have a fax for you." She turned and plucked a paper from the wire basket next to the printer. "Here you go!" With ease, she leaned over the counter, the ends of her hair sliding forward across the padded shoulders of her milky-white blouse. "Also, the folks from the lumberyard called this morning," she announced. "They'll be on the noon ferry."

Larry took the paper and glanced at the clock again. "Good! I'll meet them as soon as they arrive."

Becky sidled up to her husband and silently scanned the typed information while Judi watched the couple. His military-style crew cut made him seem that much more in command, and she thought, yet again, how fortunate Becky must feel.

Looking pleased, Larry neatly folded the sheet of paper into a perfect square and slid it into the back pocket of his jeans. "The new camp buildings are moving according to schedule."

"Ahead of schedule, actually," Becky corrected with a smile. She turned to Judi. "Thanks to a wonderful secretary who doesn't mind keeping the contractors on their toes."

"Someone has to keep them in line," Judi answered with feigned sternness. "And I'm sure Larry is ready for a full and accurate accounting." She gave Becky a knowing glance and then dutifully looked at Larry expectantly, waiting for the barrage of questions sure to follow.

Larry retrieved a small pad of paper from his shirt pocket and flipped it open. "Did the window orders make it in?"

"Done!"

"Heating and cooling?"

Judi smiled. "Done!"

"Bids for plumbing?"

"One is in and two by the end of the week." She lifted her eyebrows a fraction at his impish expression.

"Is there anything you haven't completed?"

"You act surprised!" She laughed, sitting back in her chair. "Church secretaries are always on top of their game, and in your case, on top of the construction process."

The corners of his mouth lifted into a lopsided grin. "And some secretaries are even known to keep a private stash of fudge."

Becky shook her head and laughed. "Real subtle, Mr. Newkirk."

"Your lucky day; I just happen to have a box." Judi smirked.

She reached deep into the recesses of the bottom desk drawer and pulled out the black-and-white checkered box. "You two are the only ones who truly appreciate this delicacy besides me."

Larry procured two pieces from the offered box and passed one to his wife before carefully removing the cellophane from his own piece. "If you'd just tell me where you get this stuff, I'd buy it for myself instead of pilfering from you." With practiced precision, he plopped the chocolate square into his mouth.

"Sorry," she told him with pleasure, unable to count the number of times this particular conversation played out. "It's an old family secret." Carefully, she replaced the box.

"It's not like you make it," he grumbled teasingly. "You buy it!"

"It's all the same to me!"

"What's the name of it again?" he asked.

"Angelic Hash!" She gave a mock sigh. "Really, you should write it down."

"I'll remember it next time around," he promised.

Judi knew better. He'd ask again—and again. Becky only rolled her eyes.

"So you're not going to tell where you buy the fudge?" Larry asked again, obviously choosing to overlook their amusement.

"Nope!" Judi reached around the desk and pulled out a large cylinder. "But I will give you this."

Larry caught the yellow cardboard tube she rolled across the countertop. "It's not exactly fudge, but I guess it will do."

A hollow, cannonlike thump reverberated throughout the room when he popped the top. Tightly rolled drawings spilled out into his hands as he tipped the bottom of the canister toward the ceiling. Judi watched as he unraveled and smoothed out the building plans on top of the extra desk in the outer office.

He was tall and handsome, especially on the days he wore his police uniform. All the women in the church loved him. He was gallant, caring, and most of all—handy. Not just a few women were disappointed, she mused, when he married. Actually, he and Becky were still newlyweds. Judi was happy for them—truly. They were such a good match and seemed to work together well. Since the two began working jointly on the Christian camp project, the idea of Thunder Bay went from dreams to paper to life in remarkable time. Most of all, their romance and subsequent marriage took pressure off Judi.

Larry had asked Judi out twice when she first came to the island, practically producing a spontaneous heart attack each time. It wasn't just their age difference. She had at least five years on the man. No, it had nothing to do with Larry at all. By now he probably thought her a bit odd—and rightly so. Surely Larry must have been puzzled by the contrast of her warm office demeanor versus the social ice queen act she put on to discourage all romantically inclined men.

But it had to be that way.

Judi could never date and certainly could never marry again. She drew a deep and painful breath.

Distrust ruled her life. Like an anaconda, suspicion continued to keep a constricting cord around her throat. It threatened to tighten without warning. Just seeing Larry Newkirk in his police uniform for the first time filled her with such panic she'd thought the church secretary job would have to go. Larry was working on various camp details in her church office at least three times a week. Thankfully, she concluded early on that Larry was completely harmless, saving her the heartache of finding a new job.

Besides, it wasn't just Larry. Even the most innocent probing of the church members into her personal life sent a rush of adrenaline speeding through her veins like a frenzied monster.

Still, she was free! The official documents proved it. Yet, if her mind was convinced, why did her incredibly terrified soul fail to believe? All the bases were covered—twice over. Very few could accomplish the meticulous process required to rebuild a new life, a new person. Not even the federal witness protection program promised as much.

The church phone rang, dragging her thoughts back to earth. The friendly voice at the other end offered the same weekly reminder she'd come to expect.

"I've ordered two dozen banana nut and one dozen blueberry," Lottie BonDurant announced. "Don't let Bette charge more than twenty-seven dollars. Sometimes she forgets to give the discount."

Judi promised to be diligent in her weekly pickup and quietly replaced the receiver. The ladies' Red Hat Club pickup at Bette's Bakery was the highlight of her week. The trip wouldn't be complete unless she purchased Bette's most delicate of creations for herself—the chocolate éclair. She had to laugh at Lottie. Poor Bette practically gave away the muffins at what she usually charged, but Lottie made sure the price never wavered.

Judi glanced at the clock. Ten fifteen! There was still time to get her morning work done. Situating the computer keyboard just right, she began typing again. The July calendar of events seemed filled to the brim this year, and she took special care to make sure every detail was correct. One mistake and the self-appointed editing patrol of the church would let her know—lovingly, of course. She didn't really mind. They thought their assistance was a service to Judi. Maybe it was! She grinned at the thought and hit the SAVE icon.

Satisfied the calendar was perfect, she copied the file to a disk. She'd learned the hard way about fickle church computers and lost data. Ouch! She wouldn't let that happen again. With three clicks of the mouse, she shut down the computer and gathered her pouchlike purse.

"I'll be back in twenty minutes if anyone's looking for me," Judi called over her shoulder. "Pastor's out for the morning, so lock up if you two leave."

Larry and Becky looked up from the drawings. "Muffin

run?" they asked at the same time.

A smile passed between the three. The Red Hat ladies had begun with five women, not one of them less than seventy years of age. It wasn't long before the live-wire set of old ladies had gained half the island within the group—young and old alike.

"A muffin run it is!" she answered back. With a quick wave, she disappeared through the door and into the parking lot.

&

Nathan Whithorne snapped his briefcase closed, his fingers lingering thoughtfully over the clasps. He took a deep breath and let his gaze stray to the aging metal casement window overlooking the front porch where an old wooden swing bobbed gently in the late-June breeze. The island did hold a certain charm, which he might be inclined to enjoy under different circumstances.

Suddenly exhaustion claimed his thoughts. His stomach churned at the prospect of what lay ahead, a situation he hadn't a clue how to handle. If he'd thought his heart had been ripped into shreds over two years ago when Judi died, it was now minced like crushed glass to think she was still alive. He'd loved Judi with everything he possessed. If Thomas was correct—and it blew his mind to believe it—everything in his life was about to change.

The explosive possibilities seemed mind-boggling.

Another sigh escaped as he grabbed the briefcase and shoved it into the corner. He turned to look over the quaint cabin with its smattering of easy chairs and one small sofa sitting before the dark and empty fireplace. A window air conditioner hummed steadily from the living room, providing coolness throughout the small sitting area, kitchen, and dining room. Another air conditioner was cooling the bedroom.

Nathan hadn't taken the time to look over the cabin when he'd arrived the evening before by a small commuter plane at the island airport. An earlier flight hadn't worked out, and Thomas obviously hadn't been able to secure a decent rental car deal, either. Nathan was just lucky to find any transportation to the cabin. All he wanted was a car, but the place seemed overtaken by golf carts. Traffic control, the portly man had said. But golf carts hardly seemed appropriate if it should rain, even if many of the carts were equipped with snap-on plastic windows. Who was the rental manager fooling? Plastic windows!

The small, two-door rental car he eventually found wasn't much better than the golf carts when it came to squeezing his long legs into the cramped compartment. It reminded him of days long ago when his only method of travel was his younger sister's bike—complete with a banana seat and sissy bars. There's nothing quite like pedaling in the knees-to-chest position on a girl's bike.

Now they were adults, each choosing different paths. His sister, Laurie, was the managing editor for a newspaper in Pittsburgh, and the youngest, Jeffrey, was becoming a very rich computer guru. As the oldest, Nathan had chosen to use his law degree in politics. All his desires revolved around making the world a better place. Easier said than done, he'd soon learned. Politics slowed the course of progress with enough roadblocks to discourage even the most valiant men and women.

Then there was Judi! She'd served as his legal assistant for a year while he worked for a prestigious attorney group, handling the nuisance business law cases no one else wanted. Not long after, he'd acquired favor with one of the partners and landed several challenging cases—and respect within the legal community.

It wasn't the media-covered cases he'd won nor the notoriety soon gained that he remembered most. No, his memory always ricocheted straight to Judi. Within that year, they'd fallen madly in love. Both anticipated a less than enthusiastic welcome from his family, but neither was prepared for their volatile reaction.

"The woman's not of your station!" his mother claimed with all the sensibilities the patrician lady could muster. It didn't seem to matter that their own family hadn't always been so upper-crust. Truth be told, they weren't technically wealthy, anyway. Well-off, maybe, but not influentially rich. That was a pipe dream.

Judi, though, had come from a less-than-desirable-lineage, and Nathan's entire family seemed bent on convincing him the mismatched marriage could never work. Even his meek and mild father seemed convinced Judi would never fit into the political circles of which Nathan wished to become a part.

"You've got your sights set on being a congressman, son," his father reasoned. "We like the girl, but she is not made from hearty stock. The press will pulverize her, and you by proxy."

Not to be thwarted, the couple eloped. The strategic move proved to be disastrous—for they might have won the battle with his family, but not the war. Irreparable damage was the result. His family felt betrayed; hers disappointed. No matter what Judi or Nathan did to restore family harmony and blessing, the two did not fit comfortably into either world. Judi's father had been somewhat forgiving, but not Nathan's. An evident cool chill prevailed during the Whithorne family gatherings and when given the chance, obvious slights. Even the Christmas spirit failed to relieve the tension. Nathan could still see the hurt in Judi's eyes when the family Christmas card arrived in his name alone with the expensive gold address label pronouncing his family's verdict of judgment.

Judi claimed her faith would see her through and often went to church to find solace. Repeatedly she urged Nathan to come with her and he did, but not regularly. He just couldn't make a connection with God the way she did. It wasn't until her death when he'd felt totally devoid of purpose that he chose to seek God. Then Nathan dove in headfirst to erase the pain of his loss. Between his election to the Pennsylvania House of Representatives and church, he had little time to dwell on what might have been.

Now looking back over the past two days, he had begun to reevaluate what these events meant. For if Judi's death was a farce, maybe this God-thing was a farce as well. Real Christians didn't fake their deaths and leave loved ones behind to flounder in their grief. The woman had a brokenhearted father to consider. The idea of anything so heinous was beyond his grasp.

Even now, like a vivid on-screen movie, he could see the riverbank where Judi often went to read or meditate. That horrible day she disappeared, the only thing left on the bank was a set of house keys, a half-empty bottle of water, and a book, facedown on the pages she'd been reading. Her purse and every other personal possession remained untouched in the house.

Police had noted the area where she slipped in, marking every gash in the mud where her bare feet and clawing fingernails failed to stop the fall. A piece of torn cloth from her favorite green skirt was found snagged on a nearby tree branch protruding from the broken wall of rocks. To make matters worse, several days of rain had produced rising waters and swift currents.

Authorities questioned Nathan concerning Judi's ability to swim. Oddly, he didn't know. He should have known, but the subject never came up and they'd never been in a pool deeper than three feet. Couples in love weren't interested in swimming laps.

Rescue teams dredged the Susquehanna River for two days.

"I'm sorry," the sergeant had said to Nathan. "We've not been able to find your wife."

Reliving those words still caused his chest to burn. The police presumed Judi's body would eventually surface. It never did!

But Judi's presence didn't feel lost. Wouldn't he know if she were dead—wouldn't he sense it? Family and friends assured him the reaction was natural, especially since there was no physical evidence to touch and hold. Healing would come, they promised.

It wasn't until months later when he went through her jewelry that he discovered the missing heirloom brooch. The multistoned ruby pin had been one of Judi's most cherished belongings—besides her 1972 sunflower-yellow Volkswagen Beetle. How they'd argued over that car and the high cost of maintenance the old rattletrap generated. When faced with her death, though, the arguments suddenly proved to be frivolous and stupid. Unable to part with this close link to her life, the car remained unmoved in his garage.

A seed of doubt, however, was planted the day he realized the missing jewelry piece was nowhere to be found. Riddled with suspicion, Nathan eventually asked his trusted aide to make a search. Nathan had to find closure and smother these uncertainties.

Instead, his fears became real!

Nathan glanced up at the rooster clock in the kitchen. Ten forty-five! Time to go. If Thomas was correct, Judi would be arriving at Bette's Bakery in twenty minutes. Pulling the keys from his dress pants, he smoothed his tie and gave one last look around the room before opening the door. Sun spilled into the doorway and he casually slipped on his sunglasses. He was determined not to give in to the dread streaming through his body.

The drive was short to the lakeside shops called Levitte's Landing. Tourists were crawling all over the place, and Nathan found it difficult to find a parking space.

"Plenty of time!" he said aloud, pulling the small car into a tight end spot toward the back of the lot.

Quickly, he made his way up the long aisle, his leather shoes scratching across the hot pavement. Finally, he reached the concrete walkway. Bette's Bakery was straight ahead. One shaded bench beckoned as the perfect perch from which to watch. Nathan slowed his pace and sat down, pinching up the pleats of his pants as he did so. Leisurely, he rested his back against the painted wood and waited.

Several customers entered the bakery, and he almost missed the lady in the bright pink flared skirt and white silky blouse. Her smooth strawberry hair bounced as she walked briskly by the retail shops and headed for the bakery. Nathan leaned forward.

He was tempted to remove his glasses but dropped his hand when he realized she was looking his way, her own hand trying to block the bright sun in her eyes. For a moment she hesitated and seemed to take notice of him, but eventually turned away.

Nathan's heart began to pound with full force. It was her! The squeezing sensation in his chest made it hard to breathe. He let his eyelids close tightly for a second and quickly snapped them open again. When he looked up, the door to the bakery was closing behind her and the pink of her skirt vanished inside.

Several minutes passed and he wondered if time ever crawled as slowly as it did now. Then she reappeared, once again looking his way. He stood quietly and smoothly slid his sunglasses off in one fluid motion.

The eyes of his wife suddenly locked with his.

"Long time, no see," he remarked with impressive airiness. His head tilted defiantly. "Surprise, darlin'!"

two

Judi Rydell tensed and immediately felt her hackles rise when she spotted the well-dressed man sitting on the bench outside the bakery. Plagued by an earlier uneasiness, her level of alertness was rapidly escalating.

Something wasn't right! Prior to entering the store, she had taken time to momentarily scan the crowd of tourists to find the source of her apprehension. What had she seen or heard? Nothing appeared amiss throughout the contiguous sun-drenched walkways.

Even the nearby bench had been empty when she'd glanced about—or had it? Panic made her stiffen as she glanced back at the man now sitting there. In a split second, the stranger stood resolutely to his feet, and alarm coursed through her every nerve ending. Her eyes opened wide.

Like fast-drying concrete, her feet abruptly stopped and the three shopping bags full of boxed muffins slammed painfully against her legs. Her breath stuck solidly between her constricted lungs and throat.

There was no mistaking the identity of the strikingly tall man as he effortlessly removed his sunglasses and spoke. "Long time, no see." His mouth twisted determinedly. "Surprise, darlin'!"

Nathan!

The prickle of terror churning within rapidly turned into an outbreak of sweat droplets across her forehead. Paralyzed, she could only stare back at the pair of defiant gray eyes. She stiffened again. *Help me, Lord!* The whispered prayer barely squeaked past her lips.

Nathan stepped forward and she began to jerk back, but her feet remained firmly planted. She couldn't even let go of the bags clenched so tightly in her hands.

"What?" his deep voice taunted cruelly. "You don't recognize your own husband?"

Judi went cold. What she wouldn't do for a trapdoor to swallow her whole. Matter of fact, this would be a fine time to check out of the horrendous situation with an elaborate fainting spell like the heroines in those sappy novels, yet she knew even the most contrived luxury of unconsciousness would never happen for her. No, life would force her to be cognizant of every miserable second.

Unprepared! She felt utterly unprepared. After months of readiness, her preparation for such a moment had been stymied by the calm she'd experienced on the island. His impeccable shirt and tie routine didn't help matters. He always dressed the part when he meant business, and right now the solemn expression on his face indicated every last fiber of his being was dead serious.

Biting back the fear, Judi cast Nathan an anxious glance. "What are you doing here?" she blurted.

He looked stunned at her question and laughed—a heartless, unamused laugh. Then his jaw squared and his eyes turned into chipped ice. "You're unbelievable! I come to Bay Island to find my supposedly dead wife and all you can say is 'What are you doing here?'"

"Yes!" she retorted, suddenly finding the strength to react. "It's a perfectly good question. I don't know how you found me, but it seems counterproductive to what you've always wanted."

"Counterproductive to what *I've* always wanted?" Nathan repeated with contempt. "If you're trying to confuse me, it won't work!" His expression, however, told a different story. Judi knew the compressed lines in his forehead verified the perplexity he felt.

"What did you expect, Nathan?"

His gaze traveled slowly over her. "A good story perhaps. You have no amnesia tale or kidnapping conspiracy to bombard me with? No inconsolable tears of bewilderment?" When she gave no reaction, his face inched closer. "Maybe you do surprise me."

Judi flushed but stood her ground. "You have no right to be here."

"Really!" Slowly his hand reached out and she flinched as he touched her hair. "Red hair with the blended shade of creamy milk and strawberry." When he switched his gaze back to her face she saw anger simmering beneath his cool exterior. "But changing your hair and name does not change the fact that you're still my wife, Mrs. Whithorne. Do you have any idea what you've put me through?" He shook his head at her. "You have a lot of explaining to do—a very lengthy and detailed discussion concerning your death and miraculous recovery." He leaned closer still. "Will it be your place or mine?"

She took a quick step back and felt the strands of her loose hair cascade from his hand. "I'm not going anywhere with you!"

"No?"

"No!"

Both of his shoulders lifted with impatience, and Judi braced herself for his fuming. "That's fine with me!" His voice rose a degree. "We can air our dirty laundry right here." He swept a wide arc with his hands toward the passing tourists. "They don't know me from Adam, but not so for you. How will the good folks of Bay Island react when they learn about your past? And you, a church secretary, too!" He gave her a sharp look. "I could also drag you to the island police station. You're smart enough to know it would take only one call to let this faked-death scam explode all over you."

Looking at his grim face, she knew he would make good on his threat. What she didn't know was why. Why search for her? Why come for her at all? Visions of Pastor Taylor,

Larry and Becky Newkirk, and Tilly Storm raged through her tumultuous thoughts. What if she called his bluff? Would her newfound friends understand her previous actions, the acts of a desperate woman?

"Still thinking?" he asked with deceptive laziness.

Judi felt unwell. "I don't want to go with you."

"No big revelation in that sentiment, is there?" His eyebrows shot upward sardonically. "For reasons which only you know, and I intend to discover, you went to great lengths to abandon me."

Fingers numb from the heavy muffins, she shifted the bags slightly. "I can't talk now," she argued. "The ladies are waiting on the muffins."

"Muffins!" he boomed and an incredulous expression crossed his facial features as he glanced down at the packages. He lifted eyes dark with bitterness and annoyance. "You're up to your pretty little neck in trouble and you want to deliver muffins?"

Judi screwed her lips into a frown. "The ladies are expecting me and if I don't show up soon, they'll send a search party." She eyed him with more courage than she felt. "If you want to talk, we'll talk; but I have to stop by the church first."

He seemed to consider her proposition and finally jerked a nod. "Good enough! But we go together."

What choice did she have? As if to ensure her compliance, she felt his hand lightly guide her arm.

He looked down at her, his voice quite calm. "Where's your car?"

"Cart," she corrected and swallowed nervously. "I'm parked at the far end." She pointed toward the ten-foot lighthouse replica near the entrance to the shopping center.

He said nothing more as she struggled to keep up with him. Her mind raced ahead. What was she to do? She could have easily refused to accompany him or even screamed her fool head off as a means of rescue, but he held a mighty sword over her. Those she'd come to care about, and even love, would be devastated by her deception. The important question remained unanswered—what did he want?

Judi reached her golf cart in a daze and absently pulled a set of keys from the pocket of her skirt.

"Nice set of wheels," he commented, rolling his eyes.

Feeling her face flush, she bit back the retort so close to her lips. What did Nathan know about financial struggles? With great effort, she contained herself. "It's what I can afford."

He lifted one eyebrow a fraction and seemed to consider her. "I'm taking exception to the mode of transportation, not the model." He looked over the golf cart and frowned. "Does anyone on the island own a car?"

"Of course!" Judi countered impatiently. "Golf carts are not only easier on fuel but traffic congestion, as well—especially during the height of tourist season." She placed the muffins in the back compartment and sat in the driver's seat. Immediately she noticed his expression of disapproval. A touch of frustration filled her voice. "I suppose you want to drive?"

For a moment, it looked like he might push the issue, but instead he walked over to the passenger side. "Just be sure to keep this buggy on the road." He climbed in with great effort, ducking his head until he settled into the seat, his peppered hair nearly touching the roof. He turned to look at her. "If you're having any thoughts of running us over an embankment and into Lake Erie, squelch the idea. One drowning in the family is enough, don't you think?"

"Very funny!"

A muscle tightened in his cheek. "It wasn't meant to be funny."

Judi caught his hard, incisive look and her insides quaked. Quickly she snapped on the lap belt and twisted the ignition key forward. The electric engine came to life.

Nathan had aged plenty in two years. Was this the same man she had passionately loved and married? The same man who had soon realized what a liability she was to his cherished aspirations for a successful political career? Their castle-in-the-sky marriage had turned out quite different than she'd imagined. Relentless hostility from his family was difficult enough, but having Nathan turn on her had hurt more than she could endure. He had wanted her out of the picture, and she obliged by leaving permanently—what more did the man want?

"By the way," he asked, holding on to the seat frame as she entered the main road. "Do you know how to swim?"

Judi looked sharply at him. "What's that supposed to mean?"

Gravel spewed from under the wheels of the golf cart when she veered slightly off the road and onto the rocky berm. Quickly she corrected the wheel.

He frowned again. "Maybe it wasn't such a good idea to let you drive."

"What did you mean by that last remark, Nathan?" She felt her heart begin to pound. Did he intend to harm her? If he thought she would be a docile lamb going to the slaughter, he had better think again.

He gave a wry smile. "I mean, you should keep your eyes on the road."

"Not that remark!" she cut in.

It seemed to take him a moment to follow her thought. "About swimming?"

"You know very well what I meant."

Sudden enlightenment lit his face. "You think. . ." He paused, a look of skepticism now moving across his features. "You think I'm planning to toss you to the fishes in an ironic gesture of revenge?" When she didn't answer, he gave a grunt. "That's a cheap shot, Judi, even for you. I might be angry, but I'd never lay a hand on you. Never have! Never will!" He made a little move of impatience. "I didn't come all this way to settle a score."

Her face grew hot under his scrutiny. "Then why did you come?"

Silence greeted her inquiry and she drew a deep breath, unable to take her eyes from his lean, attractive face. Again, the wheels swerved off the road and once more she corrected them. She felt his burning gaze on her.

"Pull over!" he commanded with a sigh. "You're going to land both of us in the water or the briars or both."

Judi eased the vehicle onto the stony berm and set the brake. With trembling fingers, she fumbled with the clasp of the seat belt. It refused to budge.

Nathan reached over and with one flick, easily unsnapped the belt. "My visit is making you a total wreck, isn't it?"

She let the belt fall over the side and pushed herself out of the seat. "What did you expect?"

They crossed paths in front of the cart, staring at one another as they passed, and took their respective seats.

"I'm not sure what I expected from you," he answered, releasing the brake. "It's not every day a man finds his dead wife." Glancing in the side-view mirror, he edged the cart back onto the road. "We take this road until it comes to Bayshore Drive?"

She gave him a stunned perusal before nodding. "Yes."

His glance seemed to appraise her swiftly before returning to the road. "I made a point of knowing the layout of the island before I came. You know I'm a man of details."

Disconcerted, Judi turned her head away and watched the scenery pass. Although the hot sun bore down on the island, the lake provided a fresh breeze, which now cooled her skin as the golf cart pushed past the shoreline. They rode in silence for several minutes. Nathan claimed he wasn't after revenge. Claimed he wasn't here to harm her. What could he possibly want if it wasn't to even the score or worse—finish the job?

"I believe this is your church." His voice was a harsh intrusion into her thoughts.

Judi looked up to see the redbrick church come into view. Beautiful white shutters adorned the long line of windows on either side of the main doors. The roof gradually swooped toward heaven until it peaked with the church steeple. The vented tower housed a bona fide church bell and an equally impressive heavily twined rope. One pull of the cord and the deep chime of the bell would effortlessly resonate over the entire island. Sadly, a few Sunday morning sleepyheads complained to the city council last year and the bell now remained silent except for special occasions.

Nathan turned the golf cart into the gravel parking lot and deftly parked the machine near the entrance. "Shall we go in?"

She slid out. "You could wait for me here," she suggested, bending down to look at him under the roof.

"Sorry!" He swung his long legs out. "You can't get rid of me that easily—again." Grabbing all three shopping bags, he nodded toward the doors. "After you."

Judi took a deep breath and inhaled the familiar tarlike scent that multiplied tenfold on sunny, sizzling days. The church had recently oiled the stony parking lot to keep the constantly resurfacing dirt from dusting everything in its path during the windy summer months. The odor reminded her of the private swimming pool parking lot she used to cross as a shortcut to the public recreation center as a child. Other children, clad in brightly colored swimsuits, happily disappeared into the pool area through the tall multifingered, moving turnstile. Her father never had the money to afford a pool membership. Occasionally, she was lucky enough to pass through the metal gate herself if she had a dollar and could find a member-friend to vouch for her. The pool was bigger than anything she'd ever seen, its depths clear and blue.

Memories now swirled around her; smelling the mixture of chlorine, coconut suntan lotion, and tar; how the bottoms of her blue flip-flops would be black from the oiled parking lot. Several years later, the pool closed and a paving company purchased the land, filled in the cavernous indigo pool with dirt, and blacktopped over the entire area. The transition only marked another sad step in the changes she would experience between her youth and adulthood.

"Are you ready?" Nathan was asking, nodding toward the church entrance.

From the look on his face, Judi suspected it wasn't the first time he'd asked her this very same question. The brilliant sun now felt blistering and the breeze nonexistent.

She nodded and without a word they walked to the set of double doors. Cool air shot past her as she opened the door and followed Nathan to just inside the foyer. Judi stopped to push tangled hair, now damp with perspiration, from her face.

"The door to your right," she directed, still pondering what she should do next in a short, quick prayer.

When no answer popped from heaven, she once again opened the door for Nathan. As he moved through the opening, he shot her a palpable glance of caution. She knew what rattled through his brain. He was warning her to be careful with her words, knowing that within the next few moments, the future course of her life could suddenly and irrevocably be changed. She held the next playing card, but he owned the trump. Then why did her focus now haphazardly draw to his chin and its vulnerable-looking cleft?

When she finally tore her gaze from Nathan, three pairs of curious eyes greeted the two. Larry Newkirk abruptly stopped rolling up the building plans, and even the robust Tilly Storm silenced herself midsentence from an obviously intense discussion. Only seventy-something Lottie BonDurant seemed unmoved by the interruption, fidgeting about and clearing her throat unnecessarily loudly. Becky was nowhere in sight.

"There she is," Lottie announced, her rail-thin frame suddenly straightening. She moved to tidy the frilly red box hat on her head. "We thought you'd gotten lost on the way to the bakery." Her attention rapidly swiveled to Nathan and she smiled sweetly. "Now we understand why."

Judi felt herself color, a tiny pulse starting in her neck. Perplexed, she looked up at Nathan, who was giving one of his most charming smiles back at the woman.

"Yes, I'm the cause of the delay," Nathan readily admitted to the awaiting group. "I apologize for keeping Judi from her chores." His smile widened as he looked down on Judi and she felt herself grow weak. He turned back to Lottie and held out the bags of muffins. "Hope we're not too late."

"Not at all," Lottie babbled, accepting a bag with one weathered hand and waving him off with the other. Clearly she liked what she saw.

Tilly stepped forward to take the other two bags. "Didn't catch the name," she said, her strong voice taking command. Her graying hair, pulled into a bun as usual, was topped with a ridiculously ornate crimson bonnet. The flowered dress she wore hung loosely over her ample hips and amazingly matched the hat.

Nathan stepped forward and offered his hand. "The name is Nathan and I'm glad to meet you." Judi watched as Tilly let him envelop her beefy hand. "Judi and I are close family, and I'm sure you have it in your heart to forgive us for visiting awhile."

Family! Judi rubbed her bare fingers as her eyes flew to his in amazement. How could he make such a flippant statement without flinching when her heart plummeted at the thought?

Nathan answered her look with mocking amusement. "Aren't you going to introduce me to the rest of your friends?"

Overcoming her momentary speechlessness, Judi began the proper introductions. "You've just met Tilly Storm," she began with a slight smile, giving an inward groan when she saw the spark of suspicion in Tilly's eyes. *Ignore it!* Sometimes Tilly was much too perceptive for her own good. The lovable woman had the ability to save the world one individual at a time, but she could also dig her teeth in like a bulldog when needed. The heart attack she suffered the previous fall did little to slow her down.

"And you've met Lottie BonDurant," Judi continued. "She heads up the Red Hat Club." Lottie also helped in the church library and was the self-appointed muffin-supply coordinator for the Red Hatters. She was sweet and harmless unless a church business meeting ran overtime with the frivolous rantings of one elder. Then she could be quite vocal.

Judi turned to Larry and swallowed back the lump in her throat. "Nathan, this is Larry Newkirk, our very own camp builder, handyman, and local police officer."

Larry Newkirk eyed Nathan with interest as they shook hands. Judi hoped Nathan understood her cue. It wouldn't do for Larry to begin probing.

"How long are you stayin' on the island?" This question was from Tilly.

"I'm not sure." Nathan swung his attention Tilly's way. "A couple of days at least."

Tilly continued. "You're part of Judi's family? Cousins?"

"Actually," Nathan quickly responded, not missing one beat, "we're related by marriage." Judi nearly choked, but he ignored her. Tilly opened her mouth slightly as if to ask another question but clamped her lips closed when he held up a hand. "Trust me; it's too complicated to explain."

"Oh, come on, Tilly," Lottie admonished. "Don't give the poor man the third degree. You don't have time for it." She turned to Judi and Nathan. "If you'll excuse us, we're going to be late for our meeting." Lottie blew a fluttering kiss and ambled out with her bag of muffins. "Come on, Tilly," she called.

"Nice to meet you," Tilly finally said with a look of hesitancy crossing her face. "I'm sure we'll be talkin' again."

The two women exited the room with Tilly looking over her shoulder.

If Tilly said they would be talking again, they *would* be talking again. She never spouted idle words. Judi knew that couldn't be good! Tilly wouldn't rest until she knew exactly what was going on. It wasn't merely a busybody type of wondering, but an uncanny discernment when she knew something wasn't quite right.

Larry Newkirk didn't seem quite satisfied, either. "You must be the visitor who came in on the charter plane last evening. Did you have to travel far?"

"Pennsylvania," Nathan answered honestly. "Have you ever been to the Lancaster area? It's beautiful Amish country."

Larry nodded. "Spent a couple of days there before going on to Hershey. You're right—it's beautiful sightseeing and full of good Amish cooking. I hope you enjoy Bay Island as much." His glance landed on Nathan's tie. "And if you're here on business, make sure you take some leisure time to see what the island has to offer."

"I plan to do just that." Nathan gave an easy smile and looked over at Judi. "Are you ready to get started?"

Suddenly conscious that her hands were gripping the folds of her skirt, she loosened her hold. "I suppose." She turned to Larry. "I'm going to take lunch now, but I should be back in the office sometime this afternoon. Do you need anything before I leave?"

Larry seemed to mull over her words. "Everything seems to be in order for now." He looked at his watch. "I need to be on my way to meet the lumber truck at the dock. Becky's already at the camp waiting for us." Unsnapping his cell phone from the clip at his waist, he opened it and appeared satisfied it was operating. His gaze settled on Judi. "You have my cell phone number if you should need me, right?"

This drew an odd look from Nathan, but he said nothing and Judi tried to ignore the rising panic within. She endeavored to give Larry a natural smile. "If I need you, I'll call."

Larry clipped the phone back onto his belt. "Good! I'll be back this afternoon to finish up some camp work before evening duty. Later, you can help me with a few tasks. If I don't see you, I'll make sure to catch up with you on my rounds."

Judi knew Larry was uneasy. This was his way of reassuring her he would available to check on her. God bless his kind soul! Becky Newkirk was a lucky lady to have him. He cared about everyone. The thought warmed her, and yet, Larry's concern might draw unwanted attention to her predicament. How long she could keep this problem silent was anyone's guess. Nevertheless, she had to try.

"Thanks, Larry," she finally responded.

Then Nathan looked over at Larry. "I'll try not to keep her too long." A warning glance came Judi's way. "Depending on how the afternoon goes, we might be seeing you sooner than later."

three

Nathan couldn't wait for the set of double doors to close behind him. He stood for a few moments on the hot concrete entranceway. What an inquisition! The one called Tilly would bear watching. Even with that silly hat balanced unevenly on her head, determination and authority were clearly etched in her wide, muscular face. Here was a woman who knew what she wanted and evidently was used to getting her way. She'd require special handling, the same type of management he frequently used with those on the senate floor—all with a good dose of strength of mind and willpower. He'd dealt with worse.

The other old woman, the muffin lady, was more interested in blowing kisses to strange men than looking at his dossier. Total pussycat.

The police officer was another matter altogether. He seemed more than a little cautious and a bit too interested in Judi. An unwelcome thought had been niggling at his mind ever since the guy protectively made it clear he would be calling to check on Judi. Was it jealousy?

Nathan shot a glance at Judi. Of all the colliding thoughts assailing him the past twenty-four hours, not once had he considered the possibility Judi might be seeing other men. The thought set his teeth on edge. Presumed dead or not, she was still legally married. He felt blindsided by the torrent of hurt and anger the vision caused. Could she be cruel enough to add unfaithfulness to the growing list of illegal and dishonest acts she'd committed against him?

Judi looked up at him. "Did I perform to your satisfaction?" An unmistakable cynical sharpness laced her voice.

"Brilliantly!" He meant to sound equally sarcastic, but his words came out more poignant than harsh, and her emerald green eyes narrowed in what he guessed to be mistrust. What? Did she believe he was immune to the hurt she'd caused? Recovering quickly, he forged ahead. "Seems like you've made quite a few devoted church friends on the island—especially the police fellow." He drew out his last words, slowly and deliberately.

He knew they'd hit the intended target as he gauged her quick and indignant reaction.

"That *police fellow* happens to be a married man!"

Nathan leveled her with a no-nonsense look. "May I remind you the same can be said about you?"

"Just what are you insinuating?" Two angry red splotches immediately crossed her high cheekbones. "Larry's an honorable man."

"He's not the one I'm worried about."

Her mouth dropped open in protest, but she quickly snapped it shut and began walking across the gravel. Using two fingers to loosen his restricting tie, he followed her to the golf cart. His power shirt and tie had done the trick, but they were nearly suffocating him now. The noon heat cloaked him like a heavy blanket.

When they reached the cart, Judi turned to him. "You do realize," she began, her voice tight and brittle, "that I'm not the only one with something to lose?"

"Really?" What else could he lose? He'd already lost what he had thought was the love of his life and experienced the grim realities of a supposed widower. Did she really think anything else mattered as much?

"Exposing my true identity will cause a widespread scandal in the world of politics," Judi continued with a nod of her head. "It may cost you that precious high-powered career you've worked so hard to build."

Nathan returned her angry stare without wavering. "So what!"

"So what?" she repeated with skepticism before flinging herself into the passenger seat. As soon as Nathan climbed into the driver's side, she continued. "This statement from the man who spent two years living and breathing nothing more than government policy and exit polls? I don't believe your nonchalance for one minute. You're too driven to give up that easily."

"Maybe," he answered evasively. Before starting the engine he rolled his shoulders to relax the muscles that were at that very moment knotting into a solid mass across his neck. He turned to look at her. "Your place or mine?"

"You've turned into a real man of ice, haven't you?" came her bravado response, but he could tell she was shaken.

Man of ice? Hardly! But let her suppose what she wanted, to deem him a man of iron, if it gave him the tactical advantage. Judi was a bright woman and had nearly pulled off the greatest scheme of deception he'd ever encountered, if not for two tiny mistakes he'd been fortunate enough to uncover. Or would that be unfortunate? One thing he knew: She couldn't be trusted.

"Since you can't seem to decide," he went on, "we'll visit your place. I'd like to see how my other half's been living for the past few years."

She paled slightly but made no protest. When he released the brake, her hands quickly grasped the chair bars until they formed into white-knuckled fists.

The electric cart pushed forward with ease when he pressed the accelerator. In silence they sailed past the shoreline again, and he stole a glance at her stoic face. No doubt she was planning and plotting her escape. It would do her no good. No excuse or fancy explanation would make him understand how a woman could discard her husband and family to live an anonymous life.

Did she not realize the cost? Didn't she care about the devastation happening to those left behind? There had been the horrible waiting and the equally horrific conclusion that her bloated and decaying body would never be found in the river muck. Visions of her desperate fight against the currents and the inevitable moment when she would no longer be able to hold back the cold and deadly waters from entering her lungs invaded his nightmarish dreams in the late hours of darkness. Night after night, he'd desperately tried to pluck her from the swirling murky waters, only to be pulled back by an unseen force greater than his own. Her horrible screams gurgled into a deadly silence as the swirling water filled her mouth, her eyes bulging wildly in terror. Down, down, she went, until the fiendish river closed over her.

Even now, knowing she was safe and sound, the terrifying image caused his throat to tighten. He loosened the tie another inch.

Judi must have sensed his discomfort for she looked at him questioningly. Looking at her now, he wondered how it was possible to love and yet feel something akin to disgust and hate at the same time. Exactly what emotion did he feel? Was it the same emotion his mother felt when Nathan nearly died trying to hop a passing train car with his teen friends? The foolish stunt cost him a night in the hospital. When his mother arrived at the emergency room, she cried with relief and smothered him with a mammoth bear hug. Then her love turned into wrath and he endured a tongue-lashing far worse than the accident. His mother wanted to throttle him right then and there—in simultaneous fury and love.

Was that what he felt—the relief of knowing the person he loved was alive and well, yet an all-encompassing anger at the audacity that this same loved one managed to be so? Could he really believe that the woman seated beside him, his wife, was indeed a living, breathing soul? There she was in the flesh, looking quite alive, and still. . .the world believed her to be dead.

She would have liked her memorial service. Family and friends gave her a eulogy send-off unmatched by anything he'd seen. The pastor delivered a moving message; Nathan's sister, Laurie, sang a beautiful, soul-searching song; and Nathan spoke brokenheartedly of their short time together. There was the church-prepared, post-funeral luncheon where friends fondly recalled special moments and laughed at such memories. But even their laughter was shrouded in a weighty sadness that made the mind-numbing day drag on and on.

Returning home was worse. His sister stayed for a couple of days, but emptiness echoed in the halls, as well as his heart. Even though Judi had seemed preoccupied and somewhat distant several months before her *death*, she had still managed to fill the house with her presence. At the time he had been glad when Judi finally found something to occupy her time besides obsessing about his political career. She'd almost become needy. Then she was gone. *Poof!*

The North Shore Condominiums sign came into view and Nathan slowed the cart.

"To the left," Judi directed unnecessarily. Nathan knew exactly which condo she rented. She pointed to the numbered parking spaces. "Pull into forty."

Nathan did as directed.

Taking a deep breath, he clicked off the ignition and turned to her. "Shall we?"

Her expression looked anything but ready, and if he knew her as well as he thought he did, the mix of petulance and dismay meant the woman hadn't come up with a workable escape plan.

Nathan slid out of the seat and joined her on the other side of the cart. Together they walked wordlessly toward the Cape Cod–style two-story building. He trailed slightly behind as they ascended the open but roof-covered steps. Judi stopped at the top to search inside her purse, finally producing a set of keys. She gave him a brief look of ill-concealed dread when he reached the landing, a sort of last-chance-no-clemency-firing-squad resignation. She was right where he wanted her. This should have pleased him.

It didn't!

He just hoped she couldn't read his own apprehension at what lay ahead, his own insides quaking at the results—maybe even more than hers. *Always stay on top of the opponent—or be crushed,* his father had always said. The advice seemed ripe for the picking right now. And at present, he'd need all the help he could find.

&

Judi tried to still her trembling fingers as they clumsily fumbled with the door key. What was she going to do? She could feel Nathan's bigger-than-life presence right behind her—smell the all-too-familiar hint of his aftershave. How well she remembered the expensive Blue Blood scent he always wore with his power suit. Blue Blood was as much a part of the uniform as the shirt and tie. The rich sapphire, genie-in-a-bottle form sat just to the right of Nathan's solid silver catchall tray on his very masculine, solid oak dresser. Why should she remember the scene so vividly?

She tried to beat down the memories and eruption of nerves assailing her.

The dead bolt lock finally gave way and slid back. With a brief moment of hesitation, she turned the knob and let the sizable white door swing open.

Swiftly she walked through the entry, eager to move away from his nearness and into the safety of her home. The contemporary bright array of two cozy matching chairs, a sectional couch, and mission-style end tables filled the room with comfort. The wild grape scent from a previously burned candle still lingered in the air. This was her sanctuary. Bay Island had certainly profited from the bustling tourist trade, but its popularity resulted in skyrocketing property values. If not for the generosity of a church member, she couldn't have afforded the rent, let alone the furniture, on a secretary's salary.

The front door clicked closed and Judi instantly swung back around.

Nathan was slowly advancing into the room. She couldn't help noticing how tall he was or how his expensive leather shoes sank into the plush carpet. What a silly thing to note when her life was on the line. But it was hard not to be aware of Nathan—it had always been that way. He wasn't handsome in the drop-everything-and-look fashion where one might pick him out of a crowd, but it only took a brief introduction to suddenly transform him into a rugged conqueror of the world and female hearts. Yes, he did have power in that way—and he didn't even know it.

Nathan seemed to take in the surroundings before finally turning his attention to her. He remained silent, his gray eyes holding hers.

Judi frowned, a suffocating trepidation taking over. She quelled the feeling and walked to the sliding glass door leading to the balcony overlooking Lake Erie. Quickly she slid it open and turned back to him. He hadn't moved.

"Let's talk out here," she suggested, stepping out onto the deck. Already the open air made her feel less confined. She waited patiently as he walked slowly to the opening and glanced out.

He took in the sights before coming out onto the deck. With a measure of unnerving determination he slid the door closed behind him. "Whatever you want."

Judi tugged firmly on one of the padded, heavy wrought iron chairs and moved it out from the table. The uneven scraping of the chair's hefty feet across the wood deck cut through the air. She motioned for Nathan to sit. "May I get you a soda or ice water?"

He shook his head and sauntered toward the edge of the deck. She could almost understand his fascination. The condo was a great find with a beautiful view. The deck was rather large and octagon shaped—big enough for patio furniture, a gas grill, and a large stack of wood.

She watched as Nathan rested one hand on the decorative braided rope draped between each deck post, giving it a nautical look. He seemed deep in thought, and she took his distracted moments to calm herself. He might be deliberately stalling to build tension for some dramatic moment he'd planned. For the umpteenth time she wondered why he'd tracked her down and followed her to the island after more than two years.

She could only imagine what was going through his mind as he looked so intently at the rhythmic waves washing partway up the dark, sandy beach. With the glorious summer sun reflecting and sparkling off the lake, it seemed almost criminal to mar the day with such foolishness. Even the weather appeared to be asking for tranquility. As if on cue, a cool breeze wafted across the deck, making the temperature much more comfortable.

Judi brushed back a strand of hair with a shaky hand. And she waited. Finally he turned and his gaze flickered back over to her.

"You've done quite well for yourself," he said with a quick look at the water again. Then as quickly, he turned, walked back to the table, and swept his hand gallantly toward the chair she'd indicated for him earlier. "Why don't you sit here?" He then nodded in the direction of the chair on the opposite side of the table facing the water. "I'll sit over there."

"All right," she agreed, sitting down slowly. Although she knew of no advantage the seating arrangement gained him, there had to be a tactical angle other than a view of the lake. There was always a purpose to everything he did, some strategic gain. It made him a good lawyer and, no doubt, a good politician. Regrettably for her, it also made him a formidable adversary.

The other heavy chair made no sound as Nathan pulled it back—yet another reminder of how much stronger he was than she. He sat down and watched her for several seconds before speaking. Then he leaned forward. "I thought you loved me, Judi."

Judi let go of the breath she'd held in waiting and let herself slowly drop farther back in the chair in wary skepticism. She had readied herself for a diversity of angles Nathan might approach in the forthcoming inquisition, but not this opening statement. Actually, it was somewhat comical under the circumstances and she almost laughed. "I could say the same thing to you."

His eyes narrowed in obvious thought. "You're saying I didn't love you?" He sat up straighter. "Are you asking me to believe this entire escapade and new life is my fault?"

This time Judi couldn't help letting a bitter laugh escape. "From those little notes you left for me, it seems all but obvious that this escapade, as you call it, *is* totally your fault," she accused, shaking her head at the irony of his words. *Love! What does Nathan know about love?* "What I don't understand is why you've come looking for me now. I did what you asked." She spread her hands out in exasperation. "How did you put it? Oh, yes, the exact term was for me to 'move on.'"

He stared at her in amazement. "Notes?" The look on his face left no doubt he'd thought she had popped a brain cork somewhere along the way. "What are you talking about? What notes?"

Judi wasn't about to be taken in by his astonished look of puzzlement, no matter how innocent. She lifted her chin.

"Don't play games with me. I know you were the one who wrote those eloquent but threatening notes. It might have taken me some time to decipher your scheme, but I'm not stupid. And I did as you asked; I moved on. What more did you want from me?"

Nathan lightly rapped the knuckles of his loosely fisted hand on the opaque glass-topped table. Finally he leaned forward. "Let me get this straight." Two perplexed lines appeared between his straight brows. "You're saying that I wrote you some kind of threatening notes and told you to disappear. Is that right?"

Judi stood to her feet. "Don't make it sound so harmless, Nathan. You almost killed my father with your power-hungry greed." She pointed a condemning finger at him to quiet his immediate rebuttal. "And don't give me that what-a-pity-she's-gone-mad look, either. I'm not the same naive, trusting woman you married."

Nathan frowned deeply and folded his arms patiently in front of him. "I will agree with you on your last statement, but as for these wild accusations that I'm some sort of wild-eyed villain trying to kill you and your father. . .well, you'll have to produce a plot more believable than that to explain your desertion." She watched his gray eyes narrow at her. "Nice try!" He flung his hand out lazily. "And if you're the least bit interested in your father's welfare, may I suggest that your *death* almost produced what you've so ridiculously accused me of doing?"

"How dare you!" she said in a voice she hardly recognized as her own. For several palpable moments they exchanged measured glances. Judi moved behind her chair, clutching the cushioned back for strength. "I did what was needed to protect my father from you. Don't come waltzing back into my life as if I'm the bad guy. If you've come to make trouble, I'll go to the police."

"The police?" He moved a hand over his clean-shaven chin. "That might not be such a bad option. What do you think?" He cocked his head questioningly toward her.

"I think you're playing with me." Judi stared down at him. "This is all a game to you, isn't it? You've spent two years living the life you've always wanted and now you've come searching for what you've thrown away. What are you, Nathan, two men?"

"At the moment I seem to be only one—a conniving husband who threatens innocent women and their families."

Judi stared at the man she had loved so long ago and willed her heart to harden. "A statement to which I cannot disagree."

"Then we have a problem."

Something in his tone almost touched her, but she fought any sympathetic tendencies she might develop.

"Then what do you suggest?" she asked flatly.

"Just give me a moment," he replied, leaning back thoughtfully in the chair. "When in a pinch, I always think of something."

four

Nathan slapped both hands against his thighs, pushed himself to his feet, and strolled over to the wood railing. This was one fine predicament. Call him a lousy husband. . . . Maybe a negligent spouse. . . But a note-toting madman who schemed to *do in* his wife and aging father-in-law?

What he really wanted to know was how a respectable attorney and successful state representative could suddenly plunge into a made-for-television soap opera—without even trying. Taking a deep breath, he let his gaze wander. No more than three hundred feet away were a cabana house, swimming pool, and a sand-filled volleyball court with all the picturesque quality of a vacation getaway brochure. Hardly a true portrait, though, of the current situation.

Slowly he turned and leaned one hip against the post. Pursing his lips in deliberation, he aimed a probing look at Judi. His eyes rested on her light honey tan, the clearness of her bright emerald eyes, and then on the red highlights of her soft hair. The creamy strawberry coloring would take some getting used to. The pictures his assistant took didn't do justice to the luscious coloring. The high cheekbones and full lips were the same, and if her dress weren't so long, he would probably see that her knobby knees were no different, either. She'd always tried to conceal her knees even though he'd repeatedly told her how cute the bony protrusions were.

Women! What did he know? It was as if a woman never believed a man when he said their so-called imperfections didn't bother him. Could it be they didn't want to be convinced and liked to pick over their flaws?

Take Judi's height. Even though she was beautifully tall for a woman, she was also very flatfooted—another thorn in her side, she'd always said. He wouldn't have even noticed the lack of a proper foot arch if Judi hadn't gone to so much trouble to show him her wet footprints on the front walk of their home one summer day while she watered the flowers. Actually, she thought it important enough to prove it again a few months later at the swimming pool just in case he missed the significance of the first exhibition.

As far as he knew, most men didn't fuss much over their own physical flaws and didn't have the time or the energy to fuss over their wife's flat feet or knobby knees. Whether men were just wired differently to look past such things or if love blinded a poor fellow's senses, Nathan could truthfully say there were more important things in life to focus on.

There was one difference in Judi's appearance, however, he did notice. Gone were those oversized prescription eyeglasses. Most likely the thirty-four-year-old had finally taken the leap to wearing contacts, something he could never convince her to try before—not because of her looks, but for practicality. Contacts were much more sensible and convenient.

All in all, Judi did look so very different and yet the same. But for all his scrutiny, he still had a bitter problem to solve that had nothing to do with Judi's knobby knees or nearsightedness. Too bad her intentions and motives were not as visible and open for analysis.

Did she really believe the nonsense she'd told him or was the entire tale a clever ploy to throw him off balance? If this was all a ruse, he'd have to give her points for ingenuity.

"I suppose you have proof of these allegations?" he finally asked, watching closely for her reaction. "You do have the notes?"

Indecision flitted across Judi's face. "Do you think I'd show you the evidence if I had it?"

Nathan shrugged. "You've asked me to believe that you faked your death to save yourself and your family from a person who wrote you menacing notes. Since I know that I'm not the one guilty of threatening you, then I have to determine whether to believe what you've said, misguided as it might be, or whether you're handing me a line to save your own skin." He looked at her for a long moment. "Now, will you please answer the question? Did you save any of these supposed threatening letters?"

"I have every one of those letters if you must know!" Then as if challenging him, she shook her head and loosened one hand from the back of the chair to point a finger at him. "And the letters are safely tucked away. So don't get any ideas."

Nathan blew out a frustrated breath between his lips. "Then how do you propose we resolve this problem?" When she remained still and silent, he went on. "You seem to be close buddies with that friendly island policeman. Maybe you would like to have him stand guard while we look at the letters? We could even show the letters to him if you'd like."

Something akin to panic sparked in Judi's eyes, and he could see the conflicting wheels of thought churning across her face. Just as he thought! Her reaction lent credence to his previous theory that his wife was lying. If the letters were true, why hadn't she just gone to the police in the first place? Why pull off such an elaborate charade? Wouldn't the most obvious course of action be to contact law enforcement or someone she trusted? That's what he would have done. And then there was this skittishness, which erupted every time he mentioned the police. There had to be something behind that, too. Maybe she didn't want the truth to come to light.

Or was it this particular police officer? What was his name? Larry something—Larry Newkirk. Yes, that was it. The one who was attentive—too attentive. *Don't go there again, pal*, he chided himself. That line of thought would only serve to agitate the already tumultuous waters and would be of little help with the problem at hand.

It wasn't as if he really wanted the police involved, either. The implications of Judi faking her death would be enough to rock the Pennsylvania Statehouse right off its cornerstone and down Commonwealth Avenue. If Judi publicly accused him of threatening her, there was no limit to the extent of explosion the scandal would cause. This kind of publicity he didn't need.

"Well?" He knew there was a trace of annoyance in his voice. "What do you want to do?"

An insolent light gleamed in her eyes, but he refused to back down and met her stare head-on. He could wait her out—all two minutes of it.

"I'll show you the letters," Judi announced at last, ending the standoff. Her inflection was filled with indignation, but also fear. "I don't suppose you'd be foolish enough to pull anything funny in a bank full of people." She looked at her watch. "Then we'll see what you have to say when the hard proof is right in front of you. With everything in the open, maybe we can have an honest discussion and you'll level with me as to why you're here."

"I'm all for honesty," he agreed, regarding her steadily. "And if these letters really *are* in a safety deposit box, I would like to go read them—right now. Let's put all the cards on the table."

"One condition!" Judi shifted her feet and gripped the chair again.

Nathan drew an impatient breath. The woman was deliberately hedging for time and trying to stretch his endurance. He kept his voice composed and deceptively calm. "And what would that be?"

"You may look at the letters, one at a time, but I won't allow you to take any with you, not even one." She stood poised for a second. "If you try to take anything, I'll bring the bank employees running and blow this whole thing sky high."

"Anything else?" This was turning into nothing less than a stage show.

She inclined her head in silence and did not answer. Not immediately. Instead she looked somewhat lost for a moment before responding. "If I think of another condition, you'll be the first to know."

"Glad to hear it," he returned dryly, walking past her to the sliding glass door. Deftly he slid it open. "Ladies first."

Judi turned a pensive glance to the lake waters before stepping around him and inside. Nathan wasn't quite sure, but he thought he heard a whisper of what could have been a prayer. *Good for her,* he thought; *she's going to need all the prayers she can get if this is all a lie.*

&

"Hello, Judi," greeted the smiling bank clerk when Judi stepped up to the teller window. "How's your day going?"

"Just fine," Judi answered with a fixed smile, curling her hair behind one ear. After exchanging what she felt to be necessary pleasantries, she cleared her throat. "I'd like to get into my safety deposit box."

"Certainly!" The young clerk first glanced at Nathan before nodding toward another counter to the left near the large gated door guarding the bank vault. "Meet me over by the sign-in sheet." The woman grabbed a large dangling set of mismatched keys that jingled noisily as she slid down from her chair.

Judi smoothed down her full skirt as she walked to the brown-paneled counter, well aware that Nathan was right beside her. He was being unusually quiet and that concerned her. The ride over did nothing to calm the nerves plaguing her since his arrival, and she wondered again if showing Nathan the letters was wise. If she was right, *and she was*, Nathan knew exactly what each note said. But she was safe in the bank. The safety deposit boxes were kept in a barred but partially open room. One shout was all it would take.

Still, she hoped she was doing the sensible thing. A tight little cord knotted in her throat as she reached inside her purse. The tiny manila envelope felt smooth between her fingers as she withdrew it from the inside pocket. Slowly, she tipped the envelope and let the key slide out into her other hand then laid it in front of the clerk.

"Number 243," she told the waiting teller in low tones, tilting the numbered key for her to verify.

Again, the smartly dressed young woman gave Nathan another perusal. "Let me find your card."

Judi scrutinized the clerk as she opened a large box and speculated that this woman was already falling under Nathan's spell—without him even saying a word. How could the man not know how much he affected women?

Several three-by-five cards were flipped forward until the clerk plucked one out and gave it a close look. "This is your first time accessing the box." There was a note of surprise in her statement, but she shrugged and placed the card in front of Judi. "Just sign your name and date it on the first line."

Judi did as instructed and slid the card back across the counter.

"Come on back," the clerk directed, swinging open the half door attached to the counter. "The gentleman will be accompanying you?" she asked politely.

Judi looked up at Nathan's solemn face and gave the clerk a reassuring smile she didn't feel. "Yes."

The clerk turned around, popped a large skeleton key into the lock, and the bolt slid back with a loud clang. The heavy barred door creaked open, and Judi followed the bank teller to the boxes. Finding the numbered box, the clerk stopped to inspect the ring of bank keys, trying three before finding the right match.

"Got it!" the clerk proclaimed in triumph. She took Judi's key and twisted both sets until the little metal door released. "These can be tricky at times." She paused. "Will there be anything else?"

Feeling slightly dazed, Judi just shook her head.

"That will be all for now," Nathan spoke for the first time, picking up the slack. His mouth suddenly softened. "Thank you for your help."

"You're welcome." The clerk flashed him a curious smile before turning back to Judi. "The door will automatically lock behind me. Buzz the doorbell when you're finished and one of us will come to let you out."

Judi watched as the heavy door banged shut behind the clerk and the security device clicked loudly.

Alone!

Judi blinked nervously, feeling the silence envelop her like a sealed tomb. The room suddenly felt chilly.

Nathan's voice cut through the quiet. "Do you want me to lift the box?"

"No." She threw him a swift glance and took a steadying breath. "I can reach it."

When Nathan stepped back to allow her room, she slid the box from the compartment and carried it to the waiting table, her instantly cold fingers resting on the lid. A frigid shiver of apprehension feathered across her skin. She hadn't seen or touched the letters since placing them in the box two years ago. The thought of resurrecting this appalling segment of her past weighed heavily on her mind.

She had hoped to never face the nasty accusations and threats again, but here she was, conscious of the growing and searing pain around her fearful heart. Even the deposit box repulsed and burned at her very being, and her fingers impulsively recoiled in agitation and disgust.

"Are you all right?" demanded Nathan, his hand tightly

gripping her arm as he guided her less than a foot away to sit in the worn, straight-backed chair to which she sank like a lead-based bottle. Instantly, he was looking down at her with concern, his anger momentarily postponed. "You're beyond pale and completely white."

"Nathan—" Avoiding his narrow, probing glance, she turned her head and made an effort to move her arm out of reach. "I can't do this." When he slackened his hold, she slumped back in the chair. How she hated the contents of the box that sat before her like an uncommuted death sentence. How she hated her weakness showing in front of Nathan. But rattled or not, she would not be fooled by his contrived concern. She couldn't!

"Judi, what's going on here?" he asked, obviously altering his position to look at her more fully. Suddenly there was realization in his smoky gray eyes. "You really do have some kind of horrible letters in this box."

Judi stiffened. "You know it's true."

He didn't answer right away. He seemed to consider the matter. Without waiting, he lifted the flat lid, ignoring her halfhearted attempt to block his hands, and snatched the folded brown note on top. Quickly, he spread out the wrinkled sheet between his fingers.

Judi watched as he paced the room, his eyes flitting across the page he held at arm's length, his brows creased deeply in concentration. He stopped and leaned his back against the flat wall of deposit boxes before looking back at her.

"I don't understand." Nathan was frowning heavily. "What does the note mean?" He began to read the note aloud. " 'I smell a rat. A dirty rat. Have you caught the smell of this rodent in the air? Remember The Olde Village Inn.' " He paused a moment to look at her questioningly before reading on. " 'Move on before this rat's demise is your own.' "

She felt numb, yet her throat ached fiercely and her eyes

pricked with threatening tears. That menacing note had been particularly bad. It had come right before Christmas, expertly gift-wrapped with expensive decorative foil paper. Figuring Nathan had left her an early present, she'd eagerly torn off the paper and opened the equally decorative box.

What greeted her when she lifted the lid sent her reeling. A swollen, dead rat, crawling with maggots, lay exposed. The sender had carefully wrapped the rodent in a sealed bag meant to burst open with the box lid, immediately spewing all its filthy, revolting sights and smells.

"Judi?" Nathan's voice drew her back. "What's this letter about? What does the writer mean regarding the Olde Village Inn and a rat?"

Judi drew a ragged breath and closed her eyes as tiny tears squeezed through her already damp lashes. "A dead. . .rat accompanied the note."

When she looked up, he was leaning over her, both hands on the table, his face a mixture of shock and puzzlement. She knew he was waiting for further explanation. When she remained wordless, his mouth opened to speak, but he slowly retreated instead, tapping the letter against his hand. Finally he shook his head and exchanged the note for another in the box.

Once again he paced and studied the letter, thrusting one hand into his pocket. " 'Sugar and spice isn't always so nice—is it?' " he read aloud. " 'Especially when a good Amish girl, her head full of curls, has her hand caught in the till. What a beautiful mug shot!' " Again his brow lifted in bewilderment when he turned to her.

"That was the first letter to come," Judy struggled to explain, her lips trembling, "right after the person filled the gas tank of the Volkswagen with sugar."

"What!" Nathan's glance clung to her like hot oil. "You never said anything about this letter when that happened."

"I tried to tell you it was more than a prank," she reasoned, endeavoring to ignore the confusion and anger battling in his voice.

"Judi," he went on, "don't you think I would have taken it more seriously if you would have shown me the letter? Vandals out for kicks don't leave mysterious notes behind, especially ones sounding like personal vendettas." He quirked an eyebrow knowingly. "So that leaves me to assume that you wouldn't, or couldn't, show me these notes for two possible reasons. Either you suspected—why, I don't know—that I was threatening you, or the author knew something and was holding this information over you—a blackmail of sorts."

Judi couldn't avoid his direct gaze. His quick perception of the situation petrified her. He was right, of course—except in opposite order. She didn't suspect Nathan until later. She closed her eyes in a supreme effort to calm the wild fluttering of nerves racing through her.

"I can see that at least one, or possibly both, of my assumptions are on target," Nathan assessed with annoying self-confidence.

"I tried to make you see, Nathan. . . ." Her voice trailed off nervously. "Then I had proof that you were the one sending the letters."

He stared at her in amazement. "What could possibly make you think I'd sent you these types of threatening notes along with vandalizing your car and presenting you with a dead, vile rat?" He tossed an agitated hand into the air. "First off, the handwriting is nothing more than cursive scrawl. I have flawless print!" Then as if carefully weighing an opening statement in front of a jury, he cocked his head thoughtfully in her direction. "I may not be a poet, but the grammar and hacked prose could be improved upon by a five-year-old. At least give me more credit than that."

Judi struggled to keep a flush from creeping up into her

cheeks as he threw a frustrated glance to the ceiling.

"Another thing," he went on, landing his gaze back on her. "If I'm as compulsive about every detail as you've always claimed, I can assure you that I wouldn't be able to create such a cheap product."

A hot protest rose in her throat. "You would if you were trying to disguise your handwriting. So not everything you've said is quite true. You don't *always* print, Nathan."

"What do you mean?"

"There are times when you write in cursive," Judi continued, "and no matter what you claim, your script writing is worse than scrawl. That's why you prefer to print." She lifted her chin. "And the cursive writing matches closely enough to raise a valid question."

"The *only* time I write in cursive is to sign my name," he argued. "How could you match the writing with only a signature?"

Squaring her shoulders, she shifted uneasily under his scrutiny. "Not true! When you paid bills, you wrote the entire check in cursive. Remember? You always said the checks should look uniform and that meant they couldn't be done in print *and* cursive."

Nathan's lips twitched in contemplation, and he leaned back to sit on the edge of the table. He gave a low grunt at the idea. "I suppose you're right! I'd forgotten. I used to write the checks that way." The tightness of his mouth twisted into a firm line. "With the age of electronic transactions, it's no longer necessary to write checks, and it seems like ages ago. Guess I just didn't remember."

"So we're right back to the beginning," Judi pointed out. "The handwriting in those notes does look like yours."

"Now wait a minute," Nathan quickly protested, lifting himself from the edge of the table. He scooped up another letter from the box and scanned it intently. "It's really been a long time since I've written in longhand, but still, I still don't see the similarity. I mean, this writing is absolutely terrible."

Judi couldn't prevent the wry smile from forming at the corners of her mouth. "So is yours."

"This bad?" His question seemed genuine.

Her mouth pulled knowingly to the side and she nodded. "Yes."

Nathan made a face and she could tell he was fighting the idea. His fingers fidgeted with the paper in his hand and he glanced at it again. Something in the boyish confusion marking his features moved her. A dangerous spark of feeling she thought was well hidden in the depths of her contempt for the man who was her husband was beginning to surface.

Was she crazy?

Nathan gave a sigh. "I still don't see it."

"Look at each *R* and *S*. Look at the swoops on the *L*s and slant of each sentence." She watched him closely examine the style. "Trust me, Nathan. I compared the actual letters and it's close enough to be scary."

"I didn't write these notes."

She drew a deep breath, unable to take her eyes off his lean, attractive face. The cleft in his chin seemed to deepen. He looked truly perplexed.

Slowly, Nathan leaned over, imprisoning her hand under his. His face drew close and she had the instinctive feeling he was fighting between anger and some other deep emotion. "You never had anything to fear from me, Judi." There was a pause. "I loved you!"

Judi didn't miss the past tense condition of his words. He *had* loved her. "I don't know what to say," she finally replied, trying desperately to keep her voice level. It was the truth. There were no words to describe the barrenness of her heart and feelings she had at that moment.

"I say we should get to the bottom of these letters," Nathan demanded, his voice becoming steely hard. "To do that, you'll have to tell me everything—and I mean everything—you know about these letters and what this person is holding over you."

five

Nathan studied the uneven edges of the creased paper in front on him. This was the last of the threatening letters to be copied. Not a single note made sense—at least not to him. Only Judi knew the implications of the innuendos and the power these words held over her. He rested his gold-plated pen a moment.

For some unexplained reason he believed Judi was telling the truth—as she understood it. Maybe it was the fear in her eyes or the poorly hidden grip of panic lashing out against the contents of the cold metal box. Whatever it was, the woman feared for her life. Now what? He was having a difficult time defusing the fury and resentment he'd spent the last few days building.

If only she had come to him.

Yes, he had been enormously busy with the campaign, almost numb from the frenzied pace of speeches, debates, interviews, and television commercials. But he would have dropped everything if he'd known the gravity of Judi's dilemma. She should have known that! She should have trusted him.

It would be hard to calculate the emotional, legal, and even criminal consequences of Judi faking her own death. His own inattentiveness was partially to blame. Even now, he knew the enormity of the situation was beyond his own comprehension.

"We'd better hurry, Nathan," Judi whispered across the table. "That bank teller keeps looking in. I think someone else is waiting to get to their box."

With an effort, Nathan dragged his mind back to the

present. "I'm almost done." Pushing down his previously troublesome thoughts, he briefly glanced at the doorway before giving her a reassuring look. "There's no one waiting on us. Your teller buddy is just keeping an eye on you. Bay Island must be like any other small town where everyone knows everyone—and their business." It pleased him when Judi managed a tiny smile of agreement, lightening the tension. "So, what's a bank teller inclined to do if a regular customer comes into the bank with a perfect stranger and this customer wants to get into her safety deposit box for the first time in two years? The teller is suspicious—as well she should be."

Judi seemed to think this over. "You're probably right."

"Actually," Nathan said with a small smile of his own, "I think the entire employee pool has waltzed by that door in the past half hour to make sure I haven't absconded with all your jewels and worldly possessions."

"If only they knew," came her reply with a quiet but impish laugh. Her coloring was beginning to improve dramatically.

"But all the same," Nathan continued, smoothing down his tie, "I'll finish copying this last letter so we can get out of here."

Diligently he printed the last few lines and sat back in the uncomfortable chair to appraise his work. The words needed to be exact if he was to make any sense of these letters and the possible motive behind them. Carefully, he twisted the tip of the pen until the point retreated inside and then leisurely secured it into the pocket of his shirt.

He glanced at Judi, who sat solemnly across from him, and wondered if he dared risk the fragile truce they'd developed. "Judi, I know you said that you wanted all of these letters to remain in the safety deposit box, but I'd like to keep one of them."

"But why?" Alarm spread across her face.

Nathan hesitated, rubbing his thumb across the sharp edge

of his jaw. "I came here believing you had deserted me for one selfish reason or another—all of which I couldn't understand." He rested a hand on the metal box. "You believed me to be the author of these notes." Leaning forward, he caught the gaze of her guarded look, her eyes unabashedly veiled in wariness. "Can I assume we've come to some point of agreement where you might consider another explanation as a plausible alternative? We need to take a closer look at this whole thing, including the wording and handwriting. To do that, an actual sample of the letter will be necessary."

Judi surveyed him with large emerald eyes, uncertainty still lingering in their depths. "I don't know."

"It's up to you," he assured her, spreading his hands non-chalantly before her. "I do think it will help us sort out the who, what, and why of this problem. You can choose which note comes and which ones stay."

There was a measured but deep intake of air as Judi mulled over his words. "All right. One note can't make that much difference—if it should disappear." She regarded him with a narrow gaze. "For the record, though, you need to know that I'm not convinced of your innocence."

"Fair enough!" He shrugged. "I have my own reservations when it comes to your part in this death-disappearance ploy. So we're even."

Judi's brows arched a fraction.

He launched his own quizzical look her way. "But I'm willing to concede other possibilities might exist. Are you?"

"I suppose."

"That's a starting point." Instinctively, he dropped his voice a tone or two and inclined his head toward the box. "Why don't you go ahead and choose a letter. We'll work from there."

"Fine!" Determination, sprinkled with a light dusting of edginess, crept into her voice; yet when she began to reach forward to select a note, Nathan saw her hastily pull back.

Her eyes darkened in dismay as she looked up at him. "On second thought, why don't you choose one; maybe the note you were just working on."

"If you're sure?"

She nodded. "Yes, I'm sure—if you think it will help."

"I do!" Nathan cast her a troubled glance as he folded the letter and tucked it alongside the pen in his shirt pocket. Getting her to discuss the letters might be more of a challenge than he thought if she couldn't even touch them.

"Would you mind putting away the box?" she asked quietly.

Without delay, he closed the box lid, scooped it up, and slid it back into the dark, narrow cavity. The small metal door closed easily. "Are you ready?"

Judi nodded and gathered her purse while Nathan rang the bell. The ever-vigilant bank teller wasted no time in coming.

"Find everything all right?" the teller asked with a smile.

"Yes, thank you," Judi replied as the teller relocked the vault and returned Judy's key.

As they walked through the doorway and into the lobby, several heads turned their way.

Nathan leaned close. "I think we've stirred some interest," he whispered, his hand naturally resting at the small of her back to speed her along. He felt her back grow rigid and quickly let his hand drop.

Judi looked at her watch as soon as they stepped outside into the warm rush of island air. "It's almost two o'clock," she remarked with a groan. "I need to get back to the church. I'm already an hour late."

"But you haven't eaten," Nathan pointed out with logic as they walked to the golf cart. "We also have a lot of work to do. Why don't we grab a bite to eat and then discuss what we're going to do?"

"I don't think I could eat a single bite right now."

"But I could," he quickly protested.

"Well, I can't just not show up for work," she reasoned. "My job's flexible, but not *that* flexible."

"If it's bothering you, call the church and see about taking the afternoon off. They already know you have an out-of-town visitor. I'm sure they'll understand."

"I really shouldn't." There was a sigh. "It might generate gossip and I do have work to finish for the camp."

"Your policeman friend, again?" Nathan moved to unsnap a small cell phone from the holder on his belt. "Then call your friend and explain that you're tied up this afternoon. See if the work can wait until tomorrow."

There was an awkward silence. "But I've never called off before."

"All the more reason why they shouldn't mind."

Judi hesitated.

"Call him and see." Nathan flipped open the phone and turned it on. A tart musical rumba danced across the silence as the network booted up. He handed her the open phone. "I'm sure the church and camp can spare you for a few hours."

Judi placed her purse on the driver's seat of the cart and grudgingly took the phone. "Let me see if Pastor Taylor's in first."

Nathan glanced down at her as she poised a slender finger to dial. Unbidden, his memory shot back to happier times when Judi would tenderly trace the outline of his lips with those soft, silky fingertips, nearly driving him out of his mind with longing. He closed his eyes over the burning recollection.

Suddenly, the phone came to life with a loud, annoying ring and he jerked his eyes open.

For a breathless moment, Judi stared at the offending noise before pushing it toward him. "I think it's for you."

Frowning, Nathan took the phone. When he saw the caller's name on the screen, he quickly snapped the cover down.

Lindsey! That was another fine complication he would have to deal with.

"Aren't you going to answer?" Judi asked.

Nathan rested his gaze on her. "They can leave a message. I'm busy right now." There was curiosity in her eyes, but she seemed to accept his words and he went on. "So, where were we? Calling the church, I believe." He extended the phone to her again. "Let's try it once more."

Their fingers touched lightly as she reached for the phone, and he hesitated a moment before relinquishing his hold. She lifted her gaze questioningly. Again, an electronic noise interrupted, and she slowly pulled back, her hand dropping to her side.

"Sounds like the person left a message," Judi reasoned, nodding toward the phone. "Maybe you should listen to it before I call the church."

Shaking his head, he adamantly refused. "Go ahead and make your call—and do it fast before we're interrupted again."

But Judi was already looking beyond him. "Too late!"

Nathan turned to follow the direction of Judi's gaze. Instantly, he recognized the large-boned woman named Tilly he'd met that morning striding quickly across the parking lot toward them.

"Fancy meetin' the two of you here," Tilly greeted as she drew closer, her full-mouth smile embracing both of them.

"We're in trouble." He heard Judi breathe in a soft whisper.

Nathan remained silent.

"I'm glad to catch up with you, though," Tilly continued when she stopped in front of them, her purse handles swinging wildly from her arms. "The two of you are officially invited to my house tomorrow for a good old-fashioned pot roast meal." Nathan caught her piercing gaze, his own wavering slightly in surprise when she winked at him. "It would be a mighty shame for you to visit the island without me extendin' you one of my home-cooked dinners."

"That's kind of you," Nathan attempted to cut in. "But—"

"Won't take no for an answer," Tilly went on as pretty as she pleased, glancing between the two. "Just picked up the roast at the butcher shop a few minutes ago for this very occasion and it's a real beauty." She inclined her head toward Nathan with a twinkle of determination in her eyes. "I reckon you like banana cream pie?"

"Well—" Nathan must have hesitated one nanosecond too long, because Tilly instantly picked up talking where she had left off.

"I'll bet you've never had authentic *stollen* bread, either." Her mouth curved into a wide grin, and she turned her attention to Judi. "It's one of Judi's favorites. Tell him what a treat he's in for. Nothin' like a fresh, hot, steaming loaf of bread to tickle the palate."

"No one can beat your cooking or baking," agreed Judi. "But—"

"Does six o'clock sound about right for tomorrow?" Tilly asked with obviously no intention of waiting for an answer. "Judi knows the way well enough." Then a number of wide wrinkles creased her forehead as she smiled again. "Come a bit earlier and show Nathan the flower garden." Her sharp eyes swiveled back to Nathan. "It's the peak bloomin' season and somethin' not to be missed."

Judi gave Nathan a helpless look and opened her mouth to speak when Tilly interrupted for the third time.

"No need to thank me!" Tilly waved a casual hand at Judi. "Any family of yours is a friend of mine." Before anyone could protest further, she reached into her purse and brought out her checkbook. "I'd better stop jawin' and skedaddle to get my bankin' done." She turned to go and waved a happy finger. "Don't forget, now. Tomorrow at six. I'll be waitin'."

Tilly strode away with purpose and vanished into the bank,

leaving the pair alone. Then silence fell.

"What just happened?" Nathan asked after a moment, shoving a hand into his pocket as he stared at the clear glass bank doors and then at Judi.

"We've just been shanghaied, Counselor," Judi said, her lovely eyes widening in resignation. "That's what happened."

Tilly must be slicker than oil to get through my fingers like that, Nathan mused. That didn't happen too often. He didn't have time for a home-cooked meal with a woman who obviously knew how to navigate the waters to her advantage as well, if not better, than he. This posed a new question.

He drew his hand out of his pocket and rested it firmly on his hip. "What's behind this invitation?"

"My guess is she knows something's up and believes she can help." She shrugged her delicate shoulders. "It will be useless to try to extricate ourselves from the invitation—she won't give you the chance, as you can see."

"I noticed," he muttered flatly. "She's something else. I could have used her on the House Floor last week. She would have made chopped liver out of every senator and representative there."

Judi nodded in agreement, looking up at Nathan.

"Better take advantage of the lull in the action," he advised, pushing the phone toward her. "Maybe you can make the call before any other interruptions and distractions come our way."

Again Judi nodded, and he wondered what was going through her mind as she dialed the numbers and what he was going to do with all of his pent-up frustration.

&

Judi held one hand over the wild strands of hair happily taking flight as the wind sliced through the golf cart and she continued to tightly grip the seat back with the other. The wind died down as Nathan pulled into the Dairy Barn parking lot.

"I knew the church wouldn't mind your taking some time off," Nathan remarked as he parked the cart and climbed out.

"The pastor and the people at church are wonderful," she commented, sliding out of her seat. "I don't want to take advantage of their generosity."

He only nodded and she fell into step beside him as they went into the restaurant. When they had ordered and brought their food outside to the red painted picnic table, Nathan pulled out a crisp, white handkerchief to dust off the seat. Judi laughed.

"What?" Nathan bluntly asked, giving her a quick flash of annoyance as he refolded the handkerchief. "This is one my finest pairs of slacks."

"Some things never change," she replied, finding it hard to keep the silly grin off her face. She pressed her skirt close to her legs and plunked herself down on the other side of the table. "The first thing you need to learn about island life is to lose the dapper duds. We're a laid-back lot and like to go casual."

"I feel more comfortable dressed up," he defended, slipping the paper wrapper off the straw and stabbing it into the perforated lid of his cup. "People respect the starched and pressed look."

"I didn't mean to offend you," she apologized, biting her lip to keep from grinning again. Somehow she felt considerably lighter and more relaxed. "Around here, folks respect you for who you are, not what you wear."

"You like it here, don't you?" he asked, as if the idea surprised him.

She sobered, knowing how she clung to Bay Island like a climbing tea rose to a trellis. It was her home. "I absolutely love this place."

Nathan peered into the food bag, pulled out a foil-wrapped hot dog, and handed it to her. "You seem to have made a lot of friends."

Judi pushed her own striped straw into her cup, pumping it wistfully up and down. "I know this may sound strange, but starting a new life on Bay Island gave me an opportunity to change who I was—and I like the new person I've become." She swallowed the sudden lump in her throat. "And yes, I've made quite a few new friends who I'll always cherish. It will never take the place of my own family, though." A sigh escaped. "I still miss them terribly."

Nathan seemed to regard her carefully. "Really?"

She nodded pensively. "Have you kept in contact with my father?"

"Some," he answered, lifting the bun of his hamburger to inspect the contents. He moved the pickles in a symmetrical pattern and replaced the top. His gray eyes regarded her closely. "Your father never cared much for me and in some small way has blamed me for your death, so our contact has been limited." He shrugged. "But as far as I know, he's still living in the same place and doing as well as expected." One eyebrow lifted. "He took your death rather hard."

Judi felt her previous lightness slip away and guilt moving in. "And your family?"

"Mother and Father are still in good health and active as ever," he answered. "My sister, Laurie, has been promoted to senior editor and brother Jeff is seriously in love for the tenth time. Nothing new." He gave a wry smile and took a bite of hamburger.

"That's the part I hated the most, causing pain to the people I loved. It was a choice I didn't want to make." She cast a pleading look asking for understanding. "There was no other way."

"Did you think to ask God if your plan was the only way?" Nathan demanded to know, wiping his lips with the thin paper napkin.

"God?"

"You know," he went on, pointing to the sky, "the God of heaven and earth."

"I know *who* you mean," she assured him. "I just—"

"You're simply not used to me talking about Him," he finished for her. He gave her a searching look. "You'll appreciate the irony of this. After your so-called death, I turned my life over to Christ. . .mind, body, and soul. Your faith seemed so strong and just what I needed to grab on to during those agonizing days." His expression hardened. "But you probably never thought about how I might be affected by your death, did you? Not when you thought I was the devil incarnate."

"Nathan—"

"Did you ever stop to think that I might not have been the person threatening you and that I really had loved you?"

There was that past tense version of his love declaration again. Judi tensed. "I did what I had to do, Nathan."

"Without regard for what I might have to go through, the devastation of losing a wife?" he asked, taking a sip of his drink. He paused, studying her in a way she found disturbing. "I can't begin to describe to you what that felt like. Do you know what my nights have been—" He stopped midsentence, the last coming out rushed, as if he suddenly realized how transparent he was being. "Finding you alive brings more questions than answers, Judi. It also makes me wonder if my relationship with God isn't as much of a forgery as yours."

"Don't say that, Nathan," she pleaded, a fresh sense of urgency coming over her. This wasn't how it was supposed to be at all. "I've learned so much more about God since coming to the island. My faith looked strong before, but it wasn't. My view of God and my relationship with Him wasn't right. There was so much I didn't understand then." She laid an insistent hand on his arm. "It's different now! My relationship with Christ has grown to a much deeper level."

"But you're living a lie!" he pronounced, his mouth grimly

tight. His scrutiny of her face was calculating, as if he were sizing her up. "You can't say you have God and blatantly ignore His laws."

She protested. "It's not that black and white."

"What's not so black or white about it? Either you obey His laws or you don't. How do you justify it?"

"I don't," she answered. "But what could I do? Once I finally understood what it meant to have a real live relationship with God, I was in too deep to back out." Her grip tightened on his arm. "Can you understand that? What would going back to Pennsylvania do, anyway? It would have put me right back into the hands of the person writing those letters, ruined your career, and crushed our families all over again. There was no turning back once my new life began—not without serious repercussions."

"You already have serious repercussions."

"I know!"

"No." His glance swept over her. "I don't think you do."

"What do you mean?"

Nathan leaned forward, thoughtfully propping his chin on the ball of his thumb. "I mean. . .I'm engaged to be married!"

six

"Engaged!"

Judi felt her heart stop as she waited for him to say something—anything. Since Nathan's arrival earlier in the day she had endured one shock after another, but his most recent bombshell moved her world like the shuddering shift of the San Andreas Fault.

"I guess this is another complication you didn't foresee," Nathan exclaimed, his words as sharp and clean as a two-edged sword.

Judi sat perfectly still, barely breathing. "Oh, Nathan."

She heard how thin her voice sounded, but how could she stand it? Engaged to another woman! Had the thought of him seeing other women ever occurred to her? Yes; once or twice, early on. Yet, when Mrs. Judi Whithorne died and Miss Judi Rydell's identity firmly took hold, the menacing Nathan faded off into nonexistence. She had hardened her heart against the love she knew with her husband. Not once did she seek information on him or her family in fear that someone might take notice and blow her cover. There were no harsh realities to think about if her former life was erased from the books. Now, however, she was face-to-face with this previously hidden world and the lives of those affected by her *death*.

"Certainly, you understand the difficult position I've been thrust into." His gaze was indecipherable; his face set as if in stone. "What would have happened if I had already married this woman? It's inconceivable enough to think that I, a married man, am engaged to another woman. Could this be in any way fair to her? Fair to me?" He rapped an unyielding finger on the table. "Although innocent in heart, I'd be a bigamist in God's eyes. Does any of this begin to cut at your heart as deeply as it does mine?"

"I'm not a horrible, unfeeling person, Nathan," she muttered, feeling wounded. "I'm hurting inside, too. Can't you see that?" To know he believed her capable of such self-seeking, deliberate treachery and deceit was too much to endure. Yet hadn't she thought as much of him? "I'll admit, when I formed this plan, your comfort and well-being were not highly considered. After all, you were the reason for the plan." Taking a steadying breath, she rose from her seat and faced him. "You claim to know nothing of the threats, but how do I know?" She felt a rush of heat come into her cheeks. "I'm not sure what scares me more—the possibility that you're innocent or the prospect of your guilt."

Nathan gave her a long, searching look. "Finding me guilty would make it so much easier for you, wouldn't it? Then you could write me off as getting what I deserved." Judi felt her pulse quicken as his eyes darkened. "But if I'm innocent— then what? Then I've become a victim, maybe even more so than you, and at the hand of my very own wife, the one who vowed to love and cherish me until death."

Judi sank back onto the hard, unforgiving bench seat, her stomach already sinking even lower. Like a lightning-fast whiplash to the back, his words stung appallingly close to home, leaving her flesh exposed. He was right! It would be much easier if he were guilty of the crimes she'd laid at his feet. If she was wrong. . .an unbearable weight of sin lay at her door. Which scenario was right? Her whole body moaned in fear of what the answer might be. Could she have mistaken the circumstantial evidence and foolishly blundered into a wrong conclusion? She was so sure at the time. Would she never get things right. . .not during adolescence. . .not now. . .not ever?

"And what about you?" Nathan continued with force. "Did

you plan to stay alone and single for the rest of your life? Or have you already violated our marriage as part of your new life and identity?" She saw a muscle tighten in his cheek. "Maybe that's not black and white enough for you when you account to God."

Judi felt the heat and color drain from her face. "I've always honored our marriage and not once, not ever, have I broken my vows of faithfulness to you, not even after what you"—she broke off for a second—"or what I thought you had done."

His accusation burned like acid against her core. She was a woman running for her life and the lives of her family, not a promiscuous floozy on the make. What did he take her for? She knew going into this plan that she would never know another man's companionship. That was part of the sacrifice that had to be made.

They stared at one another, reluctantly squaring off into opposite corners of throbbing hurt. She knew this would be a match with no winners—only losers.

"Ah, Judi!" he suddenly exclaimed, breaking the silence in what she recognized as exasperation. He leaned forward to grasp both of her hands and held them tightly. By the intensity of his gaze, she knew he was fighting powerful emotions. "I'm trying to deal with this as best I can. I know I'm angry. I can't help feeling angry with you, with the person who wrote you those notes—even with God." His voice turned husky. "Somehow, I have to get past this anger if we're going to solve this problem." He gazed down at her hands, still tightly held by his. "We'll have to settle our trust issues to make this work."

Judi slanted a wary look at Nathan. "Exactly what did you have in mind?"

He looked up. "Prayer!"

"Prayer?"

"I don't know if my commitment to God is a counterfeit or not, but I have to give Him a try. I have to put Him to the test." His handsome face assumed a pained but determined expression. "So, from this point on, we're going to approach this problem God's way. No more deceptions, no more lies, and no more hate."

His last word sprang instantly to the forefront. Hate? Nathan hated her? If he was innocent of the accusations, she knew he had every right to detest her. Yet it didn't make it any easier to stomach. She blinked back the stinging pain at the thought.

"Agreed?" Nathan was still talking.

Judi wondered how she could stay so calm. Nathan hated her! It wasn't love motivating his concern for her. Then what— his Christian duty? Would his hate turn into revulsion once he discovered the secrets held by the letters? That she could sit across from him while he held her hands and not totally break down from the upheaval within was something she couldn't comprehend. Casually, she looked back at him. "Agreed!"

He seemed satisfied with her answer. "Then we start by asking God what we should do."

When Nathan closed his eyes and dropped his head to pray, Judi could only watch him, feeling the penetrating warmth of his hands. What she wouldn't have given for Nathan to have shared her faith during their first year of marriage. Now he was acting like the man of God she'd always wanted. Yet this man no longer loved her, and their bonds of devoted loyalty had been broken long ago.

"We need Your help," Nathan prayed as she observed with interest. "Judi didn't ask for advice before becoming this new person, and I didn't ask for Your guidance in coming to Bay Island. Then I came here in anger and for that, I need to ask Your forgiveness." He paused, and she noticed his eyelids tightened, his thick, dark lashes compressed firmly. "We don't know who to trust other than You—we can't even trust each other. Give us wisdom about how to proceed and show us whom we can consult with in confidence. This time we want to do things Your way and not ours. That might be a sticking point for both of us, but we'll do our best." Judi could hear him take a deep cleansing breath. "Help me to know if I'm doing this Christianity thing right. If I'm not, show me what I need to do. In Your Son's name, amen."

When he looked up, Judi didn't bother to hide the fact she'd been gawking at him. With a prayer like that, how could Nathan even question his commitment to God? His humble prayer was so much more than her stuffy prayer list of complaints and wants, and tenfold better than the most eloquent churchy prayers. For the first time, a seed of hope began to sprout. Although there seemed to be no good ending to their dilemma and ominous consequences would still have to be faced regardless, knowing that God was going to run the program gave her hope.

Nathan slowly released her hands and gave her a wry grin. "Better eat your food before it gets cold."

"Too late, I'm afraid," she returned with a small laugh. Surprisingly, she did feel a twinge of hunger where a cumbersome ball of worry had previously occupied. She carefully unwrapped the foil and sniffed at the cool but delicious aroma of the frankfurter buried within the butter-grilled bun.

"Here's some mustard." Nathan handed her a yellow packet. "You were never one to eat a naked hot dog."

"Thanks!" She tore off a corner and spread a strip of velvety mustard down the length of the hot dog.

Nathan was watching her over his hamburger as he prepared to take a bite. *"Bon appétit."*

She threw him a tiny smile and, swinging her hot dog up to him, touched his hamburger in a toast. *"Bon appétit."*

❧

"I know this is difficult for you, but we need to go over what is written in each of the letters," Nathan said, spreading his sheets of notes on the coffee table in Judi's living room. "If we're going to get to the bottom of this God's way, it will require knowing the whole truth."

Judi stared plainly at him from across the table, curled up in a wingback chair with her bare feet tucked under her, a cup of tea in one hand. There was a slight trembling of her hand that belied the calm look on her face, and the cup clattered faintly when she placed it on the table. "I'm ready."

"It makes sense to start with the first letter and try to track them chronologically." He looked through the small sheets of notepaper until he found his first handwritten copy. Once again, he held it at arm's length, wishing he'd remembered his reading glasses. "You mentioned that this one was sent to you around the time when the sugar was poured into the gas tank of your car. I'm assuming the good Amish girl the person speaks about is you. What does the writer mean about you having your hand in the till and a mug shot?"

Judi's gaze faltered for a moment, and he watched her gnaw slowly at her bottom lip. "Yes," she finally answered with disdain in her voice, her gaze switching to the plush carpet. "I'm the good Amish girl with the 'hair full of curls.' You already know that I wasn't born into an Amish family, but like you, we lived among the Amish in the community. I was often referred to by my schoolmates as the Amish girl because of an old-fashioned bonnet my father bought me for Christmas one year while in elementary school."

"Go on."

"The mug shot refers to a time during my youth when I tried to shoplift an especially expensive piece of jewelry from Langerton's department store." She paused long enough to look at him, and Nathan willed his features to stay neutral. "To make a long story short, I was caught and because the item was rather costly, I was sent to the juvenile center and then to court."

Nathan leaned back. "Then what happened?"

"There were the mandatory private and group classes for a year with a county juvenile corrections counselor." She pursed her lips. "I attended like I should and kept my nose clean. In return, the county cleared my juvenile record."

"Tell me about the mug shot." He made every effort to keep his voice sounding professional, much like he would when talking with a client. He knew he was a skilled interviewer who could maintain a poker face, even though the information might bounce around like an emotionally charged firecracker inside his brain—like it was right now. This professional demeanor, however, would be hard to sustain. She was his wife, not a client.

"The mug shot?" she repeated, shaking her head slowly. "It wasn't a mug shot in the real sense. It was a picture the juvenile center took for their files, that's all. They used the photos for identification to make sure the right teen, not a paid substitute, showed up for the classes."

"You're sure this is the mug shot the writer is referring to?"

"Quite sure!" she said with certainty. "A copy of the photo accompanied the note." When he tossed her a questioning glance, she quickly added, "I tore up the photo in anger. But I assure you it was the same picture."

"How do you suppose the person acquired it?" he asked. "If your record was purged, the photo should have gone with it years ago."

Judi spread her hands halfheartedly in front of her. "I honestly don't know."

"Did anyone else have a copy of the picture?"

She shook her head. "No one!" Straightening slowly, she cocked her head. "I did have an identification badge with the same picture, but I don't remember what became of it. I'm assuming it had to be turned in."

Nathan penned the information inside a black spiral-bound

notebook and looked up. "The note mentions you having a hand in the till. What do you make of that?"

"I'm afraid that refers to another unflattering time when I was seventeen." She took a sip of tea and lowered the cup a little, the slight tremor becoming more pronounced. "I was working at the Old Village Inn at the time."

Nathan fingered through his sheets. "The same Old Village Inn noted in the ugly rat letter?"

"Yes." This seemed especially hard for her. She finally put the cup down on the table, let her legs drop to the floor, and sat nervously on the edge of the chair. "I worked as a cashier at the restaurant and. . ." Clearly agitated, she popped up from the chair and wrapped her arms protectively around her waist. "I'm not proud of what I did, Nathan. You have to believe me about that."

"It's all right, Judi," he soothed, his attorney persona taking over. "Just tell me what happened."

"Here's the whole ugly truth." Her small voice quivered on an uncertain note. "For weeks I would make change for some of the customers without entering in the ticket at the time of sale. Then I would later change the server's slip to reflect lower charges by either deleting a meal, a dessert, or sometimes the entire order, and pocket the difference."

Nathan rubbed the nape of his neck in thought. How could he have been so ignorant of Judi's past? More importantly, how did this past line up with the woman he married—the woman she was today? He didn't like being deceived and made to look like a fool. Others had tried to tell him the match between them wasn't right. Could they have seen what he so blindly missed?

With effort he kept his tone even and asked, "You were caught?"

"The manager suspected me and gave me the option of quitting or being fired. So I quit."

"No formal charges or investigation?"

She shook her head. "I was lucky that time."

"Who else knew about this?"

"There might have been one or two classmates who also worked at the restaurant," she answered slowly, her mind evidently searching back in time. "I'm sure my father suspected and my brother Tony probably knew."

"Anyone else?"

"No one I can think of."

"Why did you steal the money, Judi?" He was working to keep his reaction and resentment in check, remembering his pledge to God. Still, he had to know what had motivated her to live under such an umbrella of indiscretion.

By the look on her face, it was evident Judi was looking for just the right words. "That's a hard question."

There were so many other questions he wanted to ask, each exploding through his brain like popcorn. Had Judi kept her past a secret out of shame or self-interest? What more did she have to reveal? Why hadn't she warned him before they married, especially knowing his political aspirations? A bombshell like this had the power to derail him permanently if he were unaware and not prepared for it with damage control.

"I know what you're thinking," she said perceptively. "You're not only wondering why I felt the need to steal, but why I felt the need to keep my past hidden from you." When Nathan shifted slightly, she sadly smiled her acknowledgment. "I stole because I wanted what I could never have living on a poor father's salary. Designer jeans and the latest shirts made it easier to fit into a world where I didn't belong." She gave an indifferent shrug. "I never shared my sordid past with you because I realized early in this game of life that a straight arrow like you wouldn't have given me the time of day if you had known. Besides, I had no idea someone would dig up the information that should have been expunged decades ago and use it against me."

"You thought I wouldn't understand, much less marry you," he remarked with studied civility.

"I know you wouldn't have." She frowned grimly. "Especially if you had known that I never graduated with a degree from Penn State."

Nathan narrowed his eyes. "What do you mean?"

Judi wandered over to the sliding glass door, and Nathan twisted around and followed her with his eyes. Her fingers touched the vertical blinds as she looked out at the lake, her back toward him.

"Why not make a clean sweep of my prior misdeeds?" she exclaimed, turning to face him. "This is the last thing those letters held over me." The blinds swayed lightly behind her as she let go. "I went to a nine-month secretarial school and took a mail-order class on being a legal assistant." She flung her arms in the air. "When I went to apply for the job at your law firm, I lied on the application to get the job. There was no Happy Valley and there was no four-year degree as a paralegal."

"But your skills were impeccable!"

"Impeccable, yes," she agreed. "Honest, no. There was no way I could afford to go to a real college, and a scholarship was out of the question." She gave a bitter laugh. "I wasn't the most interested or best student in high school, and no college would give a scholarship to a student with my grade point average. Instead, I studied on my own and learned everything there was to learn about being a paralegal. I had the skills and know-how, just not the degree. And I knew your firm wouldn't hire me without that little piece of paper proving my educational worth."

"Anything else?" he dared to ask, with trepidation firmly entrenched in his mind of what she might say.

"No," she answered. "I think you'll find that these three big sins are the ones recalled in one letter or another." Her voice softened as she moved slightly toward him. "I do want you to know that when I met you and then God that year, I turned my life around. I went straight after that." She clasped her hands together nervously. "I had left that past behind when we married and erased it from my memory—until the first letter arrived."

"That put you into a bind, didn't it?"

She nodded. "I couldn't come to you for help, not without revealing my past and losing everything. Your family hated me and mine was distant. If I went to the police, my secret past would be made public. There was nowhere to turn." A deep sigh escaped. "I almost decided to risk telling you after the scary bird nest letter came."

"The one mentioning how birds didn't like breathing carbon monoxide?" Nathan asked, turning slightly to sort through the letters once more.

"That's the one." Her face turned grim. "Remember when my father's chimney flue became clogged with the makings of a bird's nest and the house filled up with carbon monoxide?" When he nodded with a frown, she continued. "The clog was no accident. Someone had stuffed it under the chimney cap and blocked the shaft." She nodded toward the paper in his hand. "The letter had come two days before the incident, but I didn't understand the significance. The other letters had come *after* the deeds." She paused. "I almost came to you when I realized my father could have died and the person who wrote the notes was responsible."

"Why didn't you?"

"When I went into your office at home, you were gone. I don't know. Maybe you received a call from your campaign manager and had to leave—that happened a lot." Pressing her fingers over one temple, she lightly shook her head. "But you had been in the middle of paying the bills and left the checks lying on the desk. It was then I realized how much the writing looked like yours. When I compared the letter to your writing and it matched, things started to add up."

"That's when you started planning a way to escape?"

"What else could I do?" she pleaded. "By then, I'd realized that you had somehow found out about my past and wanted me out of the picture. But you wanted me to be the one to leave, not you. I thought it was all about your aspirations to become a U.S. senator."

"I wish you would have come to me."

"How could I?"

"You should have had a little faith in me."

"My faith in everything was gone by that time." Her eyes grew somber. "You would have wanted an explanation of the letters. Then what? Would you still have loved me after learning about my past? Would your family have let you love me?"

It took a moment for Nathan to sort out exactly what his reaction might have been. "I don't know what I would have done," he finally answered. "But I know that I wouldn't have abandoned you."

She acknowledged his answer, but her eyes told him she didn't quite believe that scenario would have played out as he said.

He tried again. "My coming here should tell you one thing."

She lifted one brow. "What is that?"

"It should convince you that I'm not the author of these letters." He thrust a hand out in front of him. "Think about it. If I had written these letters and you disappeared from the scene so nice and tidy, there would be no reason for me to come searching for you. Am I right?"

"Maybe." She seemed to think it over. "That is a logical conclusion."

"And you weren't easy to find."

This perked up her attention. "I was very meticulous in securing my new identity."

"I know!"

"Yet you found me."

"True!"

"How?"

"It's a long story."

She sat back in the chair. "That's all right. If you have the story, I have the time."

seven

Judi settled back in the chair across from Nathan. Finally, the worst of the interrogation was over. She'd spilled her guts and lived to talk about it—for now. What Nathan thought of her past was anyone's guess. His expression never changed from one of concentration and study. But he was good in that way. There were times when clients would give the most horrendous accounts of their dealings and Nathan held the same you're-in-capable-hands air people found comforting.

She found it disconcerting!

Did Nathan loathe her more than ever before? Was he repulsed and disgusted, wishing he had listened to his family? Maybe he was already envisioning the inevitable I-told-you-so party his mother would throw. If so, then she, as his wife, had done him a terrible disservice. Could Nathan be telling the truth? As he had mentioned before, if he had been the author of the threats there would be no feasible reason for him to come to Bay Island.

If it wasn't Nathan, then who did write the letters? Two possibilities sprang to mind: his campaign manager and his mother. Both disliked her! Yet neither would have access to her cleared juvenile records. She glanced at Nathan, his head still bent over the papers, organizing them for the second time into some type of order. Again, she sensed he was having trouble seeing clearly and wondered if he had been struck with the dreaded forty-and-over farsightedness that turned ordinary people into trombone players. What the man needed was a pair of glasses.

Nathan looked up, seemingly unperturbed by her stare.

"I'll tell you what," he told her, fitting the papers neatly into a folder. "I'll fill you in on how I came to find you, if you'll do two things."

She cocked an eyebrow at him. "Just two?"

He stood and stretched his back; she heard it crack, cringing at the sound. He only smiled at her reaction. "Sorry! You never did like the snap, crackle, pop unless it was in your cereal, did you? But sometimes a guy just has to loosen the spine." He looked at his watch. "We've been at this thing for several hours, which brings me to my first request. Would you be kind enough to scavenge through your refrigerator and make me a sandwich of some sort?"

"That's an easy one," she lightly answered back, still intently watching him. He was tired, she could tell, reminding her of those long days he used to put in while campaigning. "What's your second request?"

"I'll tell you all about my journey to locate a lost wife if you'll fill me in on a few details of your plan-of-escape that also seem to be missing."

"Sounds like a bargain." She moved toward the refrigerator. "Although it's just a matter of curiosity on my part, I am interested to know what bases I failed to cover."

He followed her to the kitchen counter where his glass of water was sitting, the ice now melted, and lifted it to take a drink. A droplet of condensation fell haphazardly on his tie. He brushed it away and looked back at her. "It should be more than just a matter of curiosity."

The warning tone in his voice told her he was hinting at something serious. "If you were able to locate me, then the person who wrote those notes could find me, too. Is that it?" She pulled a bag of deli ham from the fridge and two plates from the cupboard. "Not a comforting thought."

"True," he agreed solemnly, a measure of concern etching his face. "But it's something we should consider."

He did have a point. She had been so upset at his un-expected appearance, she hadn't considered that angle before. Closing the freezer door, she automatically dropped a handful of ice cubes into his water glass. "Does anyone else know why you're here?"

"Just my assistant, Thomas," he answered, his eyes following her as she opened the bread bag. "You don't need to worry about him. He's extremely good at what he does and is even better at keeping things under wraps. Then there's the fact that he came on staff after you were gone and didn't even know you."

"Then I'm sure he's safe." She took four slices of bread out and twirled the yellow bread bag shut until it formed an airtight wrap and grabbed the twist tie. She held the plastic-covered wire tie toward him. "Still losing twisty ties and eating stale bread?"

"Of course," he answered with a reluctant but slow, mis-chievous smile.

She laughed. How an intelligent, grown man could misplace every twist tie he'd ever had the misfortune to handle was a mystery. How many times the vacuum cleaner had eaten those twist ties couldn't be counted.

Judi put the finishing touches on the sandwiches and handed him a plate. "Heavy on the cheese and light on the mayo."

He murmured his thanks as he accepted the plate and grabbed his drink. Sliding her own plate off the counter and into her hand, she trailed him into the living room. Again they sat in their same places, opposite each other, only the coffee table serving as a buffer between them.

Sitting in the chair, Judi rested her plate on the makeshift lap of her legs, both feet slipped securely beneath. "Your story has to start at the very beginning," she informed him, watching him take a bite of the sandwich, "starting with the reason for your search. I'm certain there was nothing left behind to cause doubt or raise any suspicions that my death was anything but an accidental drowning. Everything went off without a hitch."

He waited to finish chewing and chased it down with a swallow of water. "Everyone was convinced; the police, your family, my family—even me."

"Then something must have happened to change your mind," she guessed, trying to read his face. "What was it? What did I leave behind?"

"It's not what you left behind," he answered, his long mouth twisting ruefully. "It's what you didn't leave behind."

Judi racked her brain. She hadn't taken anything! Her purse, keys, clothes, jewelry, makeup—they were all left behind. Not even a toothbrush was taken. "That's impossible," she finally concluded.

"You probably thought I wouldn't notice," he consoled. "Of course, I was having a difficult time dealing with your death and admit I was grabbing at straws, but you were acting very distant and peculiar before the so-called accident. So, when I noticed the ruby brooch missing, I began to have my first suspicions about the drowning."

Puzzled, Judi shook her head. "You're not talking about my grandmother's ruby pin?"

"That's the one."

"The ruby brooch is gone?"

"By the surprise in your voice am I to presume you didn't take it with you?" It was his turn to look mystified.

The brooch was missing! Judi wanted to jump from the chair and had to snatch the sandwich plate before it went flying to the edge of the cushion. "I didn't take the brooch with me. It can't be gone!"

"I assure you the pin wasn't in your jewelry box." He seemed troubled by her outburst, a wary line creasing his forehead.

"Nathan, I'm telling you; the brooch was left in the jewelry box. I never took it with me." She dropped the plate on the coffee table rather hard but didn't care and slumped back in the chair. "How can it be missing?"

He shrugged. "When the ruby wasn't there, I assumed you had taken it with you. I knew how important it was to you, being your grandmother's heirloom."

"But I didn't take it with me," she protested, her hands clutching angrily at the arm of the chair. There were only two worldly possessions she owned that meant anything—the heirloom pin and her vintage 1972 yellow Volkswagen Beetle. Both had to be left behind, but if she had known the ruby pin would be taken, she would have risked bringing it with her. She thought it would be safe with Nathan. At the very least, the brooch should have been given to her father. "This is terrible news!"

Nathan seemed at a loss. "Could you have placed it some-where other than the jewelry box? Maybe you put it somewhere for safekeeping and forgot."

"It was in the box!" She wasn't crazy. The pin was left where it had always been. It was more than just the loss of an expensive gem. It was all that was left of her grandmother and a mother she barely knew. To be motherless was difficult enough, but the less than respectable reason for her mother's departure had marked her with embarrassment and then anger throughout her childhood. *She's run off with another man*, her father explained to her one hot summer day so many years ago. She never asked again why she had no mother. It was easier to make believe her mother left unwillingly than to cope with the reality that her mother didn't care enough to take her only daughter with her.

"I don't know what to tell you," Nathan finally said, breaking the silence. He cocked his head sympathetically. "Maybe God let it happen so I would come looking for you."

Judi pulled a face at him. "God didn't come down and take it."

"I wasn't suggesting God physically came into the room and took it," he softly returned. "I only know the ruby pin was not in your jewelry box when I went through your things. It seems an odd thing to go missing. I'm only suggesting that God may have orchestrated its disappearance—*how* I don't know—to cause me to begin a search."

Nathan was right! If the pin was missing, it was missing. There was nothing she could do about it now. How ironic! She had left the ruby behind to make a clean, total break from her former life and to prevent any suspicion. Yet the ruby had started a search ending in her discovery.

"Listen," Nathan said soothingly. "We'll add the missing ruby to our list of things to resolve. We'll find it!"

She lightly waved her hand in resignation. "You're right! It's not that important in light of my current situation." What good did it do to hold on to a pipe dream that didn't exist? The jewelry brought her no closer to the mother who abandoned her at the age of four. It did nothing to keep her father from drinking away his sorrows. No power was held in the red sparkle other than what she chose to believe. Taking a deep breath, she tried to calm herself. "Tell me what happened after you found the ruby missing."

Nathan seemed to hesitate as if waiting to see if she really wanted to move on.

"It's all right," she assured, taking the plate up again in her lap to prove it. "I'm ready to hear the rest of the story."

"If you're sure, but I have to warn you that my methods of tracking might put you to shame—I'm almost as clever as you," he remarked with an impish smile.

"Really?"

"Really! I did a thorough search of everything and came up with nothing. But then I took a long shot and it paid off." He wagged a finger at her. "I knew one day your addiction to that awful Angelic Hash fudge would be your downfall."

"You can't be serious," she sputtered in disbelief. "There is no way you could have traced me from that."

He only gave her a knowing glance and took another bite of the ham sandwich.

"You're telling me that you were able to get a list of customers buying this particular fudge and with that list you found me?" He was bluffing. There had to be hundreds, if not thousands, of people who ordered that exact fudge flavor.

He held up a waiting finger as he finished his bite. "The job was daunting. Did you know that there are over seven hundred people who regularly mail order the Angelic Hash? Five hundred eighteen of them are women, and 362 of those women have been customers for more than three years. That left me with 156 women who were customers for less than three years to check on."

"You are kidding, right?"

"Quite serious." He smiled, evidently amused by her befuddlement. "If you were alive, I knew you would somehow obtain this fudge. You wouldn't risk buying it in person from the shop, though. No, you would mail order it. So that's where I started."

"Even at that," she protested, "I used the name Amanda Rydell, not Judith."

"I know. The birth certificate you acquired was for Amanda Judith Rydell." He leaned back. "It was the process of elimination that narrowed it down."

She folded her arms across her chest. "Tell me."

"Back to the 156 women," he directed. "Of those, 61 were over the age of 55 and 10 were under 25. That left 85."

"You obtained their ages?" Fascinated now, she watched him intently.

"That's where my assistant, Thomas, comes in." He gave her a knowing look. "He first was able to secure the list with a little persuasion, and he did a basic, systematic check on every female customer who ordered that particular fudge, including their ages. Then he did an in-depth search of the remaining eighty-five and eliminated several more by profession, race, and marital status over the past two years. He arrived at nine names and you were one of them. Once he perused the driver's license photos of the nine, you seemed like a good bet. Then he came to Bay Island."

"Your assistant was here?"

"He even came into the church office one day to ask directions," Nathan went on. "You gave him directions to Levitte's Landing."

"I remember him," she exclaimed, thinking back just a week ago. "Clean-cut, tall fellow with black hair."

"That was Thomas."

Judi mockingly tapped at her forehead. "I should have been suspicious. He would have passed Levitte's Landing on his way to the church from the ferry dock. He shouldn't have needed directions." She gave a mental shake of her head. "You'd be surprised, though, at how many tourists get lost on an island no more than three miles long."

"Thomas followed you around for two days." He raised his eyebrows her way. "Did you know that?"

Slowly she shook her head. "No idea!"

"He even took pictures of you outside the pastry shop."

"This is sounding more and more like an espionage flick."

Nathan smiled. "I'm quite impressed with Thomas's abilities in this area. He might be more clever than either of us." Then he sobered. "But you can imagine my shock when he showed me the pictures. I almost couldn't believe it was you, but I knew it was. What I didn't know was why."

"Which now you know."

"Yes! It's still mind-boggling."

"I know!"

He nodded meaningfully, and then as if switching gears,

placed his plate on the table and slapped his hands lightly together. "Now it's your turn. I've explained the breakthrough that brought me here. I have a few questions for you."

"All right."

"I figure you traveled to Allegheny County two times using your legal knowledge and a computer-forged court document to gain access to birth and death certificates. I'm guessing this happened in February of that last year when you were supposed to be visiting an old college roommate." He sat up straighter. "You searched for several days until you found a birth and death certificate that matched; an infant with the name of Amanda Judith Rydell. How am I doing so far?"

"Keep going."

"You obtained an official copy of this birth certificate and began to build your new identity—a false apartment address, driver's license, and even a credit card that you had the postal service forward from an apartment you never lived in to a post office box. What I haven't figured out is how you were able to gain a Social Security number." He gave her a fixed look. "It's not every day a thirty-two-year-old woman comes in for a number."

Judi nodded. "It took me a long time to figure out that logistical problem, but obtaining a legitimate Social Security number was crucial if this new identity was to work," she explained. "I had to get a job. To provide a false number would only gain me a year, maybe two at most, before the jig would be up and I'd be on the run again."

"But you came up with a plan," he remarked assuredly, regarding her with new awareness in his eyes.

"Do you remember my work with the Hampton House?"

"Of course," he acknowledged. "You volunteered once or twice a week with the developmentally delayed handicapped children and adults."

She smiled, remembering those she had come to care a great

deal about. "I came up with a plan to take one of the adult patients with me. Tracy Stecky! I took the birth certificate I'd obtained in Allegheny County and told the Social Security clerk that Tracy was Amanda and that she would need to apply for benefits soon. Since she was never able to work due to the severity of her disability, they never questioned why she didn't have a number previously." She shrugged. "Actually, it was easy."

"And unbelievably ingenious," he remarked as Judi sensed a note of wonder and then disappointment in his voice. "Ingenious, but quite illegal."

Sadly, she had to agree. "Disappearing completely required more than the law would allow."

"You've broken a number of laws—some very seriously." He drew a deep breath and exhaled slowly. "Even the federal government will be on your case with the fraudulent Social Security number."

"After the city, county, and state have a go at me," she added grimly. "I know the law well enough to easily envision the mile-long list of charges that will flow from one prosecutor to another. It should be enough to keep several of them busy for quite a long time."

"Along with the life insurance company asking for their money back," he speculated. "That might be a problem."

Judi's head jerked up and she felt a pang of hurt. "You've spent it?"

"Not exactly," he answered, taking a deep breath. "Twenty-five thousand dollars of it I gave to the Hampton House in your name. The rest is sitting in a bank account."

Judi's heart swelled with hope and fear at the same time. "You did that for me?"

"I knew you would have wanted it," he responded awkwardly. Sadness overtook his face. "I couldn't have spent a penny of the money on myself."

She sagged back into the seat. "This is getting complicated."

"I agree!" Nathan bent forward and pressed the palms of his hands against his eyes. "It might have been better if I'd never searched for you and even better if I'd never found you. It's been like opening Pandora's box."

"What you really mean," Judi clarified, "is *I'm* like Pandora's box." When he let his hands drop and looked at her with a degree of uncertainty, she could see extreme exhaustion in his eyes. "Oh, I already know it. Everything I touch and everyone I know is somehow affected by me that way. Even my own mother left, and eventually my brother took off for Florida and never returned."

"You really believe you're the cause of these events?"

"Yes," she told him quietly. "Just look at your family. Did I ever do anything to your parents? Yet they treated me like the plague." Reluctantly, she met his gaze. "And you let them." Saying the words ripped through her chest like fiery knives. It was true! Nathan always tried to soothe the tensions between them and his parents, but not once had she ever heard him defend her honor. Because he knew what everyone else knew—she wasn't good enough.

"I had no idea you felt that way."

Judi heaved a sigh. "Why is it that other people just live their lives, but I have to scratch and claw for everything?" Their eyes locked. "When I came to the island as Judi Rydell, they accepted me for who I was. I was finally free to live life as others do." A fresh wave of despondency came over her. It was a freedom that would soon end. The prospect of losing what she valued so highly hurt terribly. The very people who taught her how to truly love God and trusted her implicitly would soon find out her secret and realize how undeserving she was of that trust. It would devastate those in the church. "I'm tired of fighting life by outwitting others with tricks up my sleeve."

There was a moment of silence until he said very gently, "Then it's time you stop trying to bend life around you and begin bending yourself. Maybe you need to start trusting a little more in yourself and giving others the benefit of the doubt." When she began to protest, he stopped her. "We promised to face this thing God's way and that will require both of us to bend. I never realized you blamed yourself for your family's troubles, and I suppose I have to share part of that responsibility for not seeing this before. Besides, you're right, as a husband, my place was to protect you—even from my own family."

"Nathan—"

"Wait until I finish," he interrupted softly. "I'm convinced that with God's help, we can get through this thing." He rubbed his hands together thoughtfully. "I'm equally convinced we need to keep clear minds to continue sorting through the details of what everything means." He swiped his hand across the back of his neck. "I don't know about you, but I've just about hit my saturation level for one day."

Judi let her gaze roam over his face. She was again struck by the lines of fatigue on his handsome features, the dark five o'clock shadow accentuating his deep chin cleft, and the vulnerability of his candid gaze. Her throat constricted at the sight and more at the fierce emotions accompanying her thoughts. Love! It was love stretching out from behind the locked door of her heart. Right now, at this very moment, she loved Nathan more than she'd ever loved anyone.

"I'm going to head back to my cabin," he told her, obviously unaware of her churning emotions. He stood up. "We both need our sleep. Tomorrow morning I'll start working on a way to help you. I'd like you to go about your day as usual at the church." He looked at her questioningly. "Can you do that? Then I'll stop by and pick you up for lunch."

Quickly, she drew herself out of the chair. "Are you sure

you're okay? You look beat." Thankfully they had retrieved his car earlier so he could leave right from her place, but the truth was—she didn't want him to go. Then the words were out of her mouth before she could stop them. "There's an extra room here."

Something passed across his features she couldn't read. He shook his head. "That's not a good idea."

Disappointed, she only nodded. "It was just a suggestion. But please be careful."

He moved toward her and gave a weak smile. "I will."

When he paused long enough, she waited in hope that the look on his face was more than just concern over the situation, but concern for her. Slowly, he bent and gave her a quick peck on the forehead. "Everything will be all right."

With that he wordlessly turned around and walked to the door, closing it silently behind him, leaving Judi looking at the white decorative wood. It was as if the warmth had suddenly been sucked out of the room and left a cold, damp chill in its place. Already she missed the man whom she had previously hoped to never see again. It was craziness! She knew beyond a shadow of a doubt she still loved him, and right now it was coming at her full force. But why? Because he believed her story? Because she finally believed in him? Because he was finally stepping forward as her protector? If possible, the love she felt was deeper and more encompassing than the day they married.

And it scared her!

She was about to lose everything, even if Nathan assured her he'd find a way to fix the problem. What if he couldn't? What if she went to prison? What if God chose not to intercede? Could she bear to lose Nathan all over again?

eight

Nathan opened his laptop computer on the kitchen table and flipped it on, turning the screen away from the morning sun. It was already past eight o'clock. He should have rolled himself out of bed at his usual time three hours ago, but he gave in to the fatigue claiming his body and burrowed in for a few extra hours. A hot shower welcomed him into the day, along with a strong cup of black coffee. Still he was drained. It made him question whether Judi had awakened yet. She would be due at work in less than an hour.

He had almost called her earlier to make sure but stopped short. Last night he was having trouble keeping his eyes focused, much less his thoughts. Seeing Judi for the first time in two years brought the enormity of his anger to the forefront until it slowly gave way to a painful bout of incomprehension, protectiveness, and then—what? If he wasn't careful, he'd fall for her all over again. He could feel the old familiar draw and knew this would be a dangerous path to follow.

She'd lied to him in the past, craftily enough to whiz right under his usual radar of perception without detection. Then her death had wrung him dry. He wasn't sure he could withstand another blow. Nevertheless, she was still his wife and whatever had passed between them couldn't change that fact. He would do whatever he could to shield her from the maniac who wrote the notes—and the law, if it came to that. The price would be steep! There was no naïveté toward the outcome. He stood to lose a great deal.

The computer came alive, and Nathan pulled his glasses out from the case, resting them squarely across his nose. Much better! Yesterday would have been so much easier if he'd remembered to take them. He let his finger roll across the pad, tapping where needed until his e-mail program opened. Quickly, he scanned the mounting mail as it downloaded. One caught his attention. Thomas had written only one word late last night: Urgent!

Without waiting he flipped open his cell phone, scrolled through the numbers, and connected. When Thomas answered, he pulled his glasses off and propped them on the top of his head.

"What's up?" he asked, not bothering to identify himself.

"You got my message, sir. Good!" Thomas cleared his throat and lowered his voice. "You need to get back here right away."

Nathan heard voices in the background. "Where are you and can you talk?"

"Hold on, sir." A minute passed as the noise gradually faded until there was silence. "All right, I'm back. The Speaker of the House only gave you a one-day reprieve on the eminent domain bill. If you don't get back here by Friday, we might have to wait until the September session starts again to get this bill passed."

"I thought we had another week or two before the session was out for the summer," Nathan replied, trying to remember his calendar. His life at the statehouse already seemed like weeks ago.

"We did have two weeks," explained Thomas, "but they passed the budget yesterday, much sooner than expected."

"I missed the budget!" Nathan couldn't believe it. How many times had they haggled for weeks over one line item after another, inevitably holding up the vote until the deadline of July 1?

"We were all surprised, sir," Thomas commiserated. "But now that the budget is passed, they want to recess early. A sort of bonus, I guess, for all their hard work."

Nathan had to think. "The speaker is willing to put my bill on the floor Friday? That's two days from now."

"Yes, sir. I already told him you had a family emergency, and he's willing to keep the session open until you can get back since you are the prime sponsor of the bill—but the sooner the better. If you wait until next week, they might pressure him to postpone it until the fall or at the very least, your fellow representatives might vote against it for spite." He gave a snort. "You don't mess with their time off."

"Don't I know it!" Nathan drummed his fingers on the table. This would shove his timetable downhill like a runaway locomotive. He had no other option. "All right! I'll be back by Thursday night. Have the committee ready and in place."

"I will, sir!" Thomas assured and then paused. "How's everything on your end going?"

"Very problematical! Has anyone been asking questions?"

"Just Lindsey."

Nathan blew out a mouthful of air. "What did you tell her?"

"I told her you were out of town attending business, sir. She seemed very anxious to talk with you."

"I'll call her!"

"Anything else, sir?"

"Thomas. . ." Nathan paused a moment to gather the right words. "Things might get ugly very soon. It's imperative that you keep this matter about Bay Island out of sight until this bill is passed. The people are counting on me to protect their property rights, and the opposition's too strong to wait for others in the committee to try to gather support again in the fall. I might not be there to rally a comeback."

"What are you saying, sir? You're going to step down from office?"

"I don't think I'm going to have a choice." The words nearly stuck in his throat. All of his life he'd wanted to make a difference and finally he'd achieved the position to do it on a grand scale. If God saw fit to let him keep his post, Nathan would be most grateful, but realistically, he didn't expect it.

"Then I wish you best of luck on the island, sir."

"I need more than luck," he said. "I need God's intervention."

"Yes, sir."

"I'll call you as soon as I get back." Nathan closed the phone thoughtfully and laid it on the table.

He would have to call Lindsey. She might call his parents and have them worried enough to cause trouble. He already had his fill of trouble. Reluctantly, he opened his phone and scrolled the numbers again until her name appeared. It rang only twice before she picked up.

"Where have you been?" Lindsey scolded, her restless voice shooting through the airwaves. "I've been worried sick. You weren't at the house, and Thomas wouldn't tell me where you were."

"Everything is all right," he soothed, instantly regretting the lie. He'd promised to do things God's way and that included the avoidance of perjury, no matter how innocent. "I can't explain right now, but I need to talk with you when I get back."

"But where are you?" she asked, her voice rising with anxiety.

"I'll explain that, too, when I get home." He pulled the glasses off the top of his head and placed them on the table. "I need you to be patient."

"Why do I get the feeling that something is terribly wrong?"

"Probably because I've never been evasive with you before," he answered honestly. "Can you trust me on this?"

"I suppose," she answered somewhat hesitantly.

"I'll be home soon."

"Soon enough for our dinner engagement with my parents tonight?" There was a hint of hurt in her voice as if she already knew the answer.

"Lindsey, I completely forgot!" Nathan could have kicked himself for not placing the date in his planner. Thomas could have headed this off. It was just the beginning of the damage he was going to cause her, and he hated it. "I'm so sorry," he apologized with genuine grief. "Please send my regrets to your parents."

"I wish I knew what was going on, Nathan," she said pleadingly. "Maybe I could help."

"I know you would help if you could, but there's nothing you can do." Nathan pinched his nose between his thumb and finger. "I promise you'll understand fully when I get back and explain everything." She would understand the situation better, but he also knew she wouldn't like it.

"Can you tell me when you'll be coming home?"

"I'll be back in time for us to get together either late Friday or Saturday," he answered vaguely.

"Then I'll wait for your call," she returned with conviction. "I have total faith in you."

Nathan winced, feeling as though he'd been slammed in the chest. "I know."

"You will call when you get home?" she asked, her insecurity resurfacing.

"Promise!"

"Please be careful," she went on, "and I love you."

Another kick to the gut. "I know." He wouldn't give her the chance to question why he didn't reciprocate the words and hurriedly ended the call. "Be good. I'll call you soon."

He couldn't snap the phone closed fast enough. He felt like a total, absolute heel. Lindsey was an innocent bystander who would be crushed under when the steamroller started moving at Judi's official comeback.

It wasn't fair to her. He and Lindsey had a comfortable relationship. For his part he had no illusions of profound love for her—all of which she accepted. But he did care for the woman.

Sure, he could say the obligatory I-love-you when the situation seemed right, but it wasn't a love like he'd had with Judi. There would never be another love like that in a lifetime.

Lindsey had been the right woman at the right time. She was beautiful, smart, and exciting. Marrying her seemed the reasonable thing to do; he was lonely, his family loved her, she was good for his political career and made him feel wanted.

Only one thing had stood in his way, causing him to hesitate about setting a wedding date—she didn't believe in God. It was quite simple to her—life was life, and then it was over. Finished! One day you exist, the next day you were gone.

Nathan, conversely, couldn't reconcile the two of them living in unity with their faith, or lack thereof, at opposite poles. It probably would have never worked out in the end, but he certainly didn't want to conclude their relationship like this. He thanked God that his hesitation saved Lindsey and himself from an even more unbearable and intolerable situation. Not that the current news wouldn't be any less demoralizing to her.

His head was beginning to ache from the complexity of the moment. He'd assured Judi that with God's help he would find a way out of this problem. It was a tall order he wasn't sure could be delivered.

He took a tired breath and stood up. It would be so easy to walk away and let each of them live their lives as they had done for the past two years. He could keep his job in the Pennsylvania House, and she could continue the new life she loved. Everyone would be happy—except for God. Okay. . .he wouldn't be happy either. How could he be happy to marry the love of his life, lose her, find her again, and then leave her under such circumstances?

Slowly he walked to the bedroom and brought out his Bible. He needed a reminder of what he was doing and quick.

Turning to Matthew 6:33, he read aloud. " 'But seek ye first the kingdom of God, and his righteousness; and all these things shall be added unto you.' "

"God, I'm seeking You," Nathan prayed aloud. "I think there's a strategy to help Judi, but I want to clear it through You first. You say in the third chapter of Proverbs to trust and acknowledge You and You will direct my path. I'm trying my best to trust. If at any time the path I'm taking isn't the right one, stop me. I'll accept Your decisions as they become apparent to me." He paused to look at the ceiling and ludicrously wondered if God heard prayers better when you looked up. "I'll call my brother this morning and get the ball rolling. Look over Judi—and Lindsey. Protect them both. In Jesus' name, amen."

Why did he feel like such a fish out of water? There were so many things in life he could manage with confidence, but trusting God to handle this wasn't one of them. How long would God allow him and Judi to stand in the fire before leading them out of the flames? What if God was trying to tell him something and he didn't recognize it in time to be of help? This faith business scared him—bad. It was all well and good when life skated along on smooth ice, but a significant bump or crack in the surface could bring a person down fast.

Nathan fell into a thoughtful silence. God would help! Why did he worry so much when he knew God would hold up His end even if Nathan faltered with his own? Hadn't God delivered on other life projects with or without his help?

Besides, he did have the makings of a plan, a plan his weary mind began yesterday.

The clock chimed the half hour and he looked up. His brother would be in his office by now, probably nursing his third cappuccino. It was time to put this plan in action. Again, he took up the phone and began dialing.

"Jeff," he greeted when his brother answered. "It's Nathan."

"Man, it's good to hear your voice!" he exclaimed, and Nathan could almost hear a smile cracking across his face. "I haven't heard from you in a couple of weeks. To what do I owe this unexpected call?"

It did his heart good to hear the lightheartedness in his brother's voice. "I need your help."

"Sounds foreboding," teased Jeff. "I'm the one usually calling you for help. What can I do you for?"

Nathan envisioned his blond-haired brother sitting at his desk, feet propped on an outstretched drawer, the computer blinking before him. "I need to know if you have any computer software that can do handwriting analysis? It needs to be as professional as possible."

"Can I ask what you need it for?"

"No!" Blunt and to the point, Nathan softened his answer with a slight chuckle.

His brother gave a low whistle. "No? You sure have been acting weird and grouchy lately—almost back to normal." He laughed at his own joke. "What is this. . .a romantic handwriting analysis for you and Lindsey to see if you're compatible? I could save you the time and money. All that palm reading and personality testing is a bunch of hooey!"

"I don't need the program for a personality profile," Nathan answered, trying to hold back a smile. "This is much more serious than that."

"Then what? More statehouse stuff, amateur sleuthing to save the commonwealth of Pennsylvania?"

"In a sense," Nathan answered, knowing if he waited long enough, Jeff's curiosity would be drowned out once he started talking computer programming. "I need a software application that can read, decipher, and compare handwriting." He thought for a second. "It would have to be able to tell the difference between handwriting samples that were meant to look alike."

"That's a big order," he remarked without sounding the least bit perturbed. "So you want professional software like the police department uses to identify forgeries, but available to the public?"

"Right! Do you have it or know where I could get it?"

"It's possible," he answered somewhat distractedly, and Nathan could hear the computer keys tapping in quick succession in the background. "The question to be asked is whether a graphology program could interpret the data like a professional. Software of this caliber is usually operated in conjunction with someone skilled in the area."

"I was afraid of that."

"Don't give up so easily," his brother encouraged, the sound of keyboard movement still evident. "Do you know anyone on the Harrisburg or Lancaster police force who would be willing to help?"

"No." Nathan sighed. He had plenty of contacts, but no one he could involve without jeopardizing the situation. The words "accessory after the fact" came to mind. How would the district attorney or public feel about him not immediately reporting the fraud once he'd discovered Judi's new life? Would they consider him an accessory to this charade? "Do you know of anyone?"

"I might," he returned, his tone suggesting his mind was preoccupied with the computer. "Our sister, Laurie, might be the one to help you." The keyboard sounded furiously again. "Remember that detective story she did in Pittsburgh about a murder suspect they convicted by using handwriting analysis? If I could just find it. . ." His voice dropped off. "There it is!" he almost shouted.

Nathan tried to recall the story and couldn't. "Did this detective do handwriting analysis?"

"That's what I'm trying to find out." There was a pause. "First I have to sign up for a free trial subscription to the

online archives of the newspaper. Just give me a minute."
Another pause. "Let me read the story. . .yada yada yada—
here it is. Yes, I think you're in luck."

"You found it?"

"Yep," he answered. "I can talk with Laurie about it if you
want. I have to call her, anyway."

"Please!" Nathan exclaimed, excited that God had opened
at least one avenue. "If she thinks this detective will do her a
favor, I'd really be grateful. All I need is to match a short letter
with the handwriting on a check."

"Can do!"

"Have her call me on my cell phone and I can fill her in."

Something in Nathan's urgent tone must have triggered
Jeff's next question. "Are you all right?"

"I'm not sure," he answered honestly. "I'll be better if Laurie
can help me out."

"All right, big brother," he responded affectionately. "I'll see
what we can do."

When Nathan closed the phone, he again thanked God.
He wanted to prove beyond a shadow of a doubt to Judi that
he was not the author of these notes and possibly, possibly. . .
find the identity of the person responsible. He would need
to scan the letter and obtain an electronic copy of a few old
checks he'd written. Buoyed by the possibility of help from
Laurie, he placed the glasses back on his nose and turned back
to the laptop. Quickly, he accessed his banking records and
flipped through several secured Web pages until he reached
the copies of his old checks. It would be best to go back to the
time when the notes were written to make all things equal.

There were the checks! Gas bill, credit card payment,
mortgage—he supposed it didn't matter. Then he saw a
check written to Judi's father for five hundred dollars. He
frowned. What he'd meant as a gift to help his father-in-law
pay medical bills was met with scorn—but it didn't prevent

the old man from cashing the check, Nathan thought wryly. Mr. Porter told him in no uncertain terms he didn't need any handouts. Thankfully, Judi never knew of the fiasco. Nathan had let it go and never mentioned it.

Why he'd kept it secret he couldn't remember. His goodwill gesture flopped, but he hadn't shirked his duty. Maybe it was time Judi realized he wasn't as unfeeling as she believed. This check was as good as any to print and use for analysis. Nathan saved a copy of the check and two others in the computer. These he would send as one file.

Now, for the threatening note. With a few cable connections to the computer, he set up the portable scanner-printer and within minutes printed out the perfect copy of the note he planned to have compared. This he also saved into a file.

That was the first step. When he met with Judi for lunch, they would plan step two and try to figure a way to keep Tilly Storm from scavenging information at dinner that evening. It wouldn't be easy, but imperative. The world would rain fire down on their heads if the situation wasn't handled just right. Their lives depended on it!

nine

Judi sluggishly dropped her purse into the desk drawer and locked it. She felt depleted and knew her appearance let it show. Without purpose she sank down into the chair and plucked her hairbrush from the top drawer, running it through the out-of-control curls that looked more like a twirl of pink cotton candy on a paper stick than her usual soft, smooth waves. She'd taken a shower soon after Nathan left the night before, but was too tired for the usual blow-dry and curling iron routine. Then after a night of fitful turning in her sleep, the damp hair had turned into the Bride-of-Frankenstein beehive by morning. Wetting it down with copious amounts of gel and trying to finalize the disaster with hair spray didn't improve matters.

She gave a sour grimace at her reflection in the small mirror on her desk, sticking out a rebellious tongue at the less than flattering result. "Who cares what you think!" she demanded of the object.

Just as she figured, the mirror didn't seem to care.

Suddenly, she heard the church office door pop open and caught a glimpse of Larry Newkirk strolling in with a smile. Quickly, she dropped the brush back into the drawer and shoved it closed.

"Good morning," he cheerfully greeted as she turned toward the counter. He was dressed in his customary crisp police uniform, evidently pulling another double shift from evenings to days. The poor guy worked all the time.

"Morning," she mumbled back with as much enthusiasm as she could muster. She noticed a momentary break in his concentration when he took in her appearance, but thankfully he said nothing of it.

"Did you have a nice afternoon yesterday?" he asked politely, checking the small wooden mailbox slots in the outer office.

Judi managed a slow smile. "Yes, thank you."

"I saw your cousin coming back to the Stantons' cabin last night," Larry went on, sounding nonchalant while he opened an envelope retrieved from the mail slot. "That is where he's staying, isn't it?"

Larry was on a fishing expedition and she knew it. "No," she finally said. "I believe he's staying at the rental next to the Stantons'. The old McGreevy place."

He moved toward the counter and set the letter down. "You're sure everything's all right? You seemed a little uncomfortable yesterday."

"Just a little surprised, that's all." That was an understatement.

He gave a grim nod. "You know if you ever need help, Becky and I are only a phone call away."

"I know," she said, her smile widening. "I appreciate knowing there are good friends to rely on when needed."

The office door immediately pushed open again and Becky burst in, her face bright with excitement.

"Did you hear the latest?" Becky asked, her long black hair swishing lightly from side to side as she looked between Judi and Larry. When they shook their heads, Becky clapped her hands together in delight. "Jason and Lauren Levitte are expecting twins. Isn't that marvelous?"

"Twins!" Judi repeated in pleased astonishment. Now here was a couple God had managed to bring back together in what seemed like an impossible situation. After five years of separation, Lauren came back to the island to set right the accusations Jason had made that caused her to leave the island in the first place. Although Judi wasn't around to witness the breakup several years ago, she was there in time to see the reunion. The entire island talked about it for weeks. Finally, they married and were now expecting twins. If God could heal their botched love and hurts, maybe there was hope for Nathan and her after all.

"It's true!" Becky bobbed her head, continuing with vigor. "Won't the residents be surprised in the spring? It will be like a population explosion. I'm not sure the island has ever had three babies at one time."

"Three?" Judi asked, immediately noticing the bright shade of red creeping up Larry's neck. Becky was looking aghast and subconsciously planted a hand over her abdomen. Then Judi knew. "You're expecting, too?"

"Oops!" Becky's hand instantly flew to her mouth in chagrin.

Larry gave a lopsided, almost shy grin. "We weren't going to tell anyone yet, at least not until we had talked with our parents."

"My lips are sealed." Judi laughed, mimicking the pull of a zipper across her mouth. "But please accept my early congratulations."

"Thank you!" both said in blissful unison.

There was another of God's miracles. Becky was a missionary forced out of the Congo due to political unrest that made it unsafe for Americans. While furloughed on Bay Island, she became involved with the building project of the Thunder Bay Christian Camp and its lead committee member—Larry. They fell in love. It was a wonderful romance, blemished only by Becky's rich father, who couldn't accept her life as a missionary or as a wife to a "lowly" police officer. Her parents never even bothered to come to the wedding. Judi had met the father once—and once was enough. He was a tough egg to crack. Yet Becky mentioned how much peace God gave her over the situation, and she believed one day her daddy would come to know Jesus. That was real faith.

Even the cantankerous church elder Van Edwards seemed to find love. Judi hadn't missed the ogle-eyed looks Mr. Edwards and Tilly Storm had been exchanging the past several months. Ever since Tilly's heart attack last year, Mr. Edwards thought he was Tilly's personal trainer. It was heartwarming to see, really. Both were alone and made the perfect couple. Yes, romance and now new life were in the air on Bay Island. She hoped there would be enough romance left for another unlikely couple.

Was it possible? Maybe it was too much to ask. She would have to win Nathan back and clear herself in the bargain. There was also another woman in the picture, one Nathan loved. She'd seen God work in the lives of so many, but none were tackling the love triangle and legal battle she now faced. Was He up to the challenge?

"I need to get back to rounds," Larry finally announced to the ladies. Giving the counter a light slap with the palm of his hand, he gave Judi a pointed look. "Call if you need us for *anything*!"

"Yes, sir!" Judi gave a mock salute.

Becky laughed and gave her husband, the new daddy-to-be, a kiss on the cheek. "Isn't he handsome when he's so commanding?" She smiled back at Judi. "I need to meet the plumbing contractor at the camp, so we both better get going. We'll see you later, Judi."

Like a whirlwind that blew in, the two blew right back out, leaving Judi relieved for a quiet moment. She immediately busied herself with the ever-growing stack of paperwork and phone calls. Totally immersing herself in her familiar world of secretarial duties and tasks helped bring back a stabilizing calm to the morning.

One last keystroke completed the Sunday bulletin, and Judi pushed back her chair, critically looking at the screen text for errors. So deep was her absorption, she didn't notice Nathan enter the office until she looked up to see him standing at the counter watching her. How long he'd been there she didn't know. Immediately, she felt color rushing into her face.

"Nathan!" Judi swiveled in the chair to fully face him, wishing she could control her blushing reaction. "Is it noon already?" She looked up at the clock in surprise.

"Almost," he answered. "Are you about ready for lunch?"

"Just give me a minute!" Slightly unsettled, Judi quickly set about saving the files on the computer and rearranging the piles of papers on the desk to be finished that afternoon. She retrieved her purse and knocked on Pastor Taylor's door.

"I'm off for lunch," she announced after cracking the door open wide enough to pop her head inside. He gave his blessing with a smile and went right back to work.

"Where would you like to go for lunch?" Nathan asked when they stepped out of the building.

"There's a great taco place at Levitte's Landing," she said after some thought, smiling inside again at the reminder of the news announcing Jason and Lauren Levitte's twins. Twins! Even Jason's shopping center masterpiece couldn't compare to this development.

"That will be fine," Nathan was saying as he directed her to the golf cart. "Do you mind if we take your *'coupé de cart'*? I'm beginning to get the hang of this island transportation business. I wasn't sure at first, but it kind of grows on you."

Judi gave a light laugh at his pun and handed him the keys. "Be my guest."

By the time they'd ordered lunch and sat on the pier overlooking the boat dock, Judi was ravenous. Nathan hadn't even blinked when she ordered three tacos and must have sensed her mounting hunger for he gave a quick prayer for grace.

Judi took a hasty bite, immediately splitting the hard taco shell in two. Half of the meat and cheese contents spilled into the wrapper. The lettuce and tomatoes soon followed. "Sorry," she apologized with a shrug. "These can be a little messy."

Nathan looked at the disintegrating taco then back at her, seeming to take in her appearance for the first time. His eyes widened slightly when his glance lighted on her frizzy hair.

"Bad hair day," she explained, taking another bite of her food. The open ride to the dockside shopping center hadn't helped.

A short but deep one-syllable hum was his only response. It seemed his mind wasn't on her hair for too long—or his food, for that matter. His burrito remained untouched.

Finally he spoke. "I talked with Laurie this morning, and I think we've found someone who can analyze at least one of those threatening notes you received. I sent her a copy of the one note and three checks that I wrote during that time period."

Judi stopped eating. "You told your sister about me?"

"No," he answered, his gray eyes on her. "Laurie doesn't know the how or why of the project. That's the marvel of trusting someone—they do what you ask without questioning, even though they don't understand why."

Judi felt a blush come to her cheeks again. She wasn't sure he'd meant to zing her, but his words held a bitter sting, and behind those deep, penetrating eyes lingered a hurt she knew she had placed there with her mistrust. He was being more aloof today, and she wondered at his changing mood. For the moment she would choose to ignore the barb, if that's what it was, and move on. "What do you hope to find by having the analysis done?"

"First, it will prove that I'm not the author of the notes," he stated plainly, and when she tried to protest that she had already figured out that fact, he stopped her. "I think you'll feel better if it is in writing. The other reason is to gain information about who *did* write the letters."

"Then what?"

"Then we have to get through dinner tonight without this Tilly woman discovering who I am."

Judi scooped the meat back into the fractured taco with a plastic fork. "That will be hard to do."

"It's imperative she not find out," he insisted. "I have a very important eminent domain bill coming before the House. If anyone, especially the media, finds out about you before the vote, that bill will be dead in the water."

"It sounds really important."

"It is!" His serious, handsome eyes turned to the lake waters, a passion taking over his voice. "People are losing their land to private developers who are abusing the eminent domain laws. This bill would put a stop to that. Unfortunately, the legislative session is closing earlier than usual, and I have to be there to present the bill for a vote on Friday."

"This Friday?" Judi nearly choked on the last bit of lettuce.

He gave a solemn but decisive nod. "It couldn't be helped. The vote was due earlier, and I've already stalled it once. They won't keep the session open just for this bill, and waiting until the fall will seriously jeopardize its passage."

"That means you'll have to leave tomorrow," Judi pronounced, pointing out the obvious. "What am I supposed to do?"

Nathan took a deep breath. "I haven't worked out all the details yet, but I was thinking it might be best if you stay on the island until I send for you—maybe on Saturday. We'll need to retain an attorney, and then I'd like to gather our families together to explain the situation before going to the police. It depends upon a lot of things falling into place at the right time."

"But if I leave on Saturday, when will I get a chance to talk with those close to me here on the island?" she asked, her pulse quickening. "I can't just leave and let them find out about me on the news. What about my job? This will leave the pastor and the church in a terrible spot come Monday morning."

"I'm still working on that part," he countered, turning his face to meet hers squarely. "What's important right now is that Tilly doesn't detonate the bomb before its time."

Distressed, Judi shook her head. "I'll do my best, but you've seen firsthand how tough she can be."

"I know."

She knew Nathan was doing his best to hold the situation together with so many delicate threads of circumstance hanging in the balance, any of which could snap between now and Friday.

A deep sigh erupted within. Nathan should never have come looking for her. It was disastrous for both of them. Yet another passion pulled just as hard at her heart, if not harder, telling her she was glad he did. But what could she do about that now? If only she could just disappear again. She wondered if he'd considered the possibility and decided to pose the question. "How do you know I'll be here when you send for me?"

A flicker of surprise registered in his eyes, but his voice remained even and calm. "You'll be here," he said confidently, "because I believe you've told me the truth and there's no reason for you to run from me now." Suddenly he frowned. "You're no longer frightened of me, are you?"

"No!"

He leaned forward. "Don't you have some level of trust in me?"

"Yes."

"Then why would I think you might not be here when I send for you?" His rhetorical question seemed suspended in the air, a feather sustained only by a slight updraft. Then he added, "And I trust you, Judi!"

The conviction of his words caused two things to happen:

It kept Judi's hopes afloat that Nathan might still have some love left for her within his bruised heart, and the words caused her to rethink the risk Nathan was taking for her. He trusted her and this trust caused him to act gallantly on her behalf. Although it would break her heart to lose him again, it was extremely painful to know this allegiance might cost him everything.

"Nathan," she approached softly with her voice, daring to take his hand in hers, "you said that your assistant is the only one who knows that I'm alive and no one here knows about us. Have you considered going back to your own life in Pennsylvania and leaving me to my own here?" She looked down at his strong hands. "It might be easier that way."

"Is that what you want?"

She raised her eyes and saw that his face was very quiet and serious, his gray eyes unfathomable, as if her next words meant a great deal to him. "It's not what I want that matters anymore, Nathan. I can see how important the people of Pennsylvania are to you. They need you! Your family needs you. How can I ask you to chance all of that?" She shook her head despairingly. "Look at what it has already done with this important bill that needs to be passed on Friday. I don't want to be the one to mess this up for you or the people who are depending on you to obtain justice for them."

A slow smile crept across his face in what she could describe as relief. "We promised to do this God's way, right?" She nodded noiselessly and he continued. "Then that option doesn't exist for us."

"So what option does exist when it comes to us?" she asked, anticipating and dreading the answer at the same time. "If we're going to publicly come out with this, where do we stand as a husband and wife?"

He was silent for a long moment, and she feared he might not answer. Then he took a deep breath and met her stare.

"For now," he finally conceded with some hesitancy, "we stand together."

Judi should have known she was pushing too hard, too fast. She could feel it. Nathan was a man of action. Once the dust settled, he'd look at their marriage and determine whether it was worth salvaging or if the woman waiting in the wings was his destiny. She only hoped what was left of their love wouldn't be trampled when all was said and done.

❧

Nathan looked over at Judi in the passenger seat, her wild hair flying in the wind as she pointed to the next road. She directed him up the pine needle-covered driveway to a quaint cabin shaded by a swarm of mature trees.

"This is it," Judi declared when he stopped the cart and turned off the ignition.

Nathan glanced at her again. She'd given him a scare that afternoon with her talk about disappearing. The thought hadn't occurred to him until the moment she spoke it aloud. He supposed the possibility existed, but it seemed, at least on the surface, her thoughts of escape had been born out of a concern for him.

Then again, maybe he was being suckered. Wouldn't that be a kick in the pants? Yet, when she reached for and held his hand within hers, her forceful green eyes looking vulnerable and alive, he had wanted to kiss her—badly. But he didn't! He wanted to drive away her pain. But he couldn't! Their problems had begun well before the threatening letters were ever sent. Certainly, his feelings and even passion for her was still strong. He wouldn't, however, leave his heart exposed and bleeding again until he was sure she was through conning herself and other people. She had to be serious about sticking around to save their marriage.

Suddenly, the sound of a screen door flying open and the twang of the metal spring broke his deliberations, and he saw

Tilly racing out to meet them.

"Come on up," she said, beckoning with her hands as she quickly ambled toward them.

By the time he climbed out and was waiting for Judi, Tilly was upon them. First she gave Judi a mammoth hug, totally eclipsing the tall, slender figure. Then Tilly turned on him.

Nathan quickly held out a hand. "Thank you for inviting us for dinner."

Tilly gave a dismissing look at his hand and then barreled forward, wrapping her thick arms around him, pushing the air clear out of his lungs. "We don't stand on ceremony, honey. We're friendly people." A few swats to the back made him cough until she finally drew him back with a wide, toothy smile. He delicately tried to withdraw himself, feeling as if he'd been put through a wringing machine, but Tilly kept a tight grip on his arm. "I'm mighty glad you're here."

Nathan barely had time to catch his breath before she swept them up onto the porch landing and into the cabin.

"Sit yourselves right down and relax," she demanded, scurrying around the small living room. "Dinner is almost ready."

Tilly disappeared around the corner and into what he presumed was the kitchen. The living room opened into the dining room where a beautifully table was set for four.

Judi sat down on the small sofa and Nathan dropped down next to her, adjusting his long legs in an effort to get comfortable.

"Who else do you think is coming for dinner?" he whispered, his mouth within inches of her ear.

Judi turned toward him, but before she could utter a word, the answer appeared out of the kitchen. An older man with pure white hair and the most enormous blue eyes bulging from behind thick glasses came into the room. A frilly and quite unmanly apron was tied around his waist. A somewhat grumpy look was planted on his face.

Although Nathan was sure he'd not seen this person up close before—he would have remembered those eyes—the man did look familiar. Nathan racked his brain to place him.

"Hello, young man," the older man said gruffly, stepping forward. "I see you found the place all right." He nodded a greeting at Judi. "And you brought the missus."

Nathan stood silently to his feet, and he felt Judi scramble up beside him. An uneasy feeling settled over him, but he momentarily shook it off and held out a hand to the old man.

If possible, the elder one's eyes grew wider as he intently looked at Nathan's face and then his outstretched hand. He seemed to be taking inventory, and Nathan wondered if the old man would find him up to snuff.

When the man finally grasped his hand in a viselike grip, he blurted only two words. "Van Edwards!" Then he scrutinized Nathan's face again as if waiting to see if the name meant anything to him.

"Nice to meet you, Mr. Edwards," Nathan returned, wondering if he should recognize this man who didn't seem inclined to let go of his hand. Yet the name meant nothing. "I'm Nathan and I think you know Judi."

Mr. Edwards peered out from his thick glasses, aiming his sharp gaze at the two of them. "I know who you are, Representative Whithorne." He paused only briefly as he zeroed in on Judi. "And I know this is your wife!"

ten

Nathan stared at the old man in stunned silence until he felt Judi sway lightly against his arm, the coolness of her skin shocking him back into reality. He turned to see her colorless face and hastily placed a steadying hand around her waist, guiding her back to the couch, where she sank down without an argument. Even Mr. Edwards's eyes grew pensive when he glanced at the pale figure. Nathan straightened and, like a shield, slowly moved into position between Judi and the white-haired man, keeping both within sight.

"Now look what you've gone and done," Tilly scolded as she came into the room and took in the scene. "I told you to wait until we had finished dinner." She brushed past both men, her ample hips swishing loudly against her polyester skirt as she did. Sitting down solidly beside Judi, she threw another reproachful look at the unsmiling elder before turning her attention back to Judi. "There, there," she soothed, firmly patting her hand.

"Well, it had to be said," the old man argued, his lips firmly set.

"And I told you there had to be a logical explanation if you'd just give 'em time." Tilly blew an upward, frustrated breath that lifted the few wisps of gray hair loose on her forehead. "Now look at the poor girl. You've shaken her bad."

Nathan returned his gaze to Judi, who seemed to be thunderstruck, but recovering, and then he turned to Tilly with barely concealed anger in his voice. "What's this all about?"

Tilly in turn looked at Mr. Edwards and then to Nathan. "Now let's everyone stay calm like. It doesn't do a body a

117

bit of good to get all riled up. There's a plain and simple explanation for everything." Her head tipped toward the old man. "Van here saw you eatin' at the Dairy Barn yesterday and recognized you as the lawmaker from Pennsylvania. With a little searchin' on the library computer, we found a news piece about the drownin' of your wife whose picture was lookin' remarkably like our Judi here." She thumped Judi's hand a few more times. "Guess we kinda put two and two together."

Nathan remembered the man now. He was the one cleaning tables at the restaurant where Judi and he had eaten the day before. Knowing this made him even more confused. Why should an old man playing busboy in his retirement years recognize a state representative from another state when 80 percent of his own people in Pennsylvania didn't even know the name or face of their own representative, let alone someone not in their district? Yet this man from Ohio knew who he was.

"Are you denying that this woman is your wife?" Edwards challenged, ignoring the warning look Tilly gave him.

Nathan narrowed his eyes. "I'm not confirming or denying anything until I find out what your interest is in this matter. Tilly invited us to dinner tonight, and yet it seems more like an ambush party with accusations for the main course, apparently meant to cook our goose instead of the pot roast. I want to know why!"

"I invited you to dinner—that's what I planned and that's what you'll get," Tilly quickly interjected, shaking her head in frustration. "I love Judi like one of my own. It's just that being the observant body that I am, I noticed a slight tan mark where a weddin' ring used to be on Judi's finger when she first came to the island. I figured she'd be talkin' about it one day when the time was right." Her keen eyes gave Nathan a knowing look. "But when you came waltzin' in yesterday with her, I figured you must be the ex. Thought maybe I could help the two of you, that's all." Unperturbed, she casually took a balled-up facial tissue from her apron pocket and loudly blew her nose into it. "Findin' out about this other nonsense didn't happen until today."

"When Mr. Edwards supposedly recognized me, the two of you decided to do some investigating, is that it?" Nathan asked bitterly, not liking the story one bit.

"Tilly thinks there must be a mighty good reason why you've misled people to believe Judi's dead when she's been living right here on the island." Mr. Edwards seemed bent on being unpleasant. "Now I'm not so easy to fool."

"Please stop!" Judi stirred restlessly to the edge of the seat, seeming to rally at last. "Nathan had nothing to do with this, Mr. Edwards. This whole thing is my fault."

"Don't say any more, Judi," Nathan immediately warned, holding up a hand to silence her.

"Nathan," Tilly pleaded, hoisting herself up with effort from the couch. "Listen to what Van has to say. If you're in trouble he can help. I'm a pretty good judge of character, if I have to say so myself, and I've seen your record at the statehouse. You're a good man."

"That still doesn't tell why the two of you are so interested," Nathan reasoned, a sudden blaze in his eyes. He didn't care for Edwards's highhandedness any more than he liked Tilly's nosiness.

"First of all, young man," Mr. Edwards retorted, pointing a bent finger his way, "Judi is our church secretary. If she's not who she says she is, then I want to know the why and how of it. I don't take lightly to our church people being duped. As a church elder who has served more years on the board than you've been breathing, I have a right to know the extent of this pretense." The man squinted his eyes. "No funny stuff, either. I'm warning you to be careful with your words, and you'd better tell the truth the first time around. I won't waste any time getting Officer Newkirk over here. That boy's right smart. He'll sort this whole thing out lickety-split."

"Please, Mr. Edwards," Judi implored, scooting closer to the edge of her seat. "It's not Nathan you want, it's me."

Nathan shushed her, not so gently this time. "Let me handle this."

He needed time to think. He'd asked God to provide a path to follow and the wisdom to guide him to the right people. Then why did he suddenly feel like he was on a challenging downhill slalom course without the benefit of skis? It wasn't like there was a fork in the road where he had a choice of paths. There was only one steep and icy path, taking this trust thing with God to an entirely different level of technical difficulty—perhaps beyond his capabilities of faith. What could God have possibly been thinking to send him a grumpy old man who wore women's lacy aprons and an island busybody whose loyalties, and possibly brains, seemed scattered?

"Well," the old man groused, "what'll it be?"

Frustrated, Nathan frowned. What choice did he have? It irked him to be shoved into a cage like a cornered dog.

"It's all right, Nathan," Judi insisted with resignation. Grabbing his arm, she stood to her feet. "We have no other choice but to confide in them. If Larry comes, he might be understanding of the situation, but he would be bound by duty to take action." She lowered her voice to a hush and lifted her face close to his. "And I know Mr. Edwards. He won't back down for anything. We can only hope to pacify him long enough so you can leave tomorrow to complete what you need to do."

"You two can stop the whispering!" Edwards's blue eyes darted accusingly between the two.

"Simmer down, all of you!" Tilly shook her head vehemently. "I've about had my fill of this! Now, Van, you get off your high horse for a minute and let these young folks decide what they want to do." She turned to Nathan and Judi. "And the two of you can take a few minutes to talk over this thing while I get the food situated. I promised you a dinner and heads are gonna roll if this perfectly good roast goes to ruin."

Mr. Edwards *harrumph*ed but backed off and strode irritably back into the kitchen, paying testament to the equality of stubbornness he and Tilly possessed.

"That's better." Tilly seemed appeased for the moment. "Nathan, you take our Judi here and get comfortable at the table. Don't let the old coot scare you off." Her tone suddenly turned soft. "He's just a big ol' teddy bear on the inside."

Nathan could hardly believe the audacity and outright perjury of her words. Was the woman blind? Her "teddy bear" rivaled the great black bears roaming the countryside of his home state, and these bears were anything but cuddly. He was tempted to enlighten her about this fact, but instead turned toward the table, doing as he was told, still smoldering inside over the turn of events. He didn't want to eat, and he was sure Judi's appetite was spoiled, as well. He was sure, however, that Tilly's threat about heads rolling wasn't an idle warning if the food went to waste.

"What do you think the old-timer is up to?" he asked Judi as soon as they were alone.

"Just what he said," Judi answered matter-of-factly. "He's no lightweight and a real fighter. You should see him during the church business meetings. Only a few brave ones dare to take him on." She paused in thought. "There's also something strange about him."

"Other than the fact he's wearing a lacy apron?" Nathan couldn't help asking.

This brought a small smile to her full lips. "Other than that," she answered. "I don't know how to make sense of it, but a con artist can usually spot another con artist. You know what I mean?"

"Possibly," Nathan answered hesitantly. "Are you saying this Edwards guy is a con man?"

"Rumor on the island says that he has to work at the Dairy Barn to make ends meet. I don't buy it!"

"In what way?"

"It's hard to put into words, but things seem to happen when Mr. Edwards becomes involved."

"Things happen? Like what?"

"Take the new camp for example," Judi began. "Old man Edwards fought hard against the development of this camp for the longest time. The church was even having second thoughts since the camp committee couldn't secure the land— at least not until Mr. Edwards finally agreed the Thunder Bay Landmark might not be such a bad site for a Christian camp after all." She flung her hands out. "Then all of a sudden, the land is donated and money starts pouring in—and I don't mean hundreds—I mean thousands."

"You think he's a rich entrepreneur who tries to pass himself off as a helpless old man?"

"Maybe," she conceded.

"What about Tilly?"

Judi visibly relaxed and gave a fond smile. "She's creative and devious, but genuine. No doubt she thought her dinner tonight was going to be a matchmaking experience. She must be extremely disappointed." She gave a light chuckle. "You wouldn't believe how good she is in the romance territory— it's almost eerie. With Tilly on your side, you can't go wrong."

"She seems nosy to me."

"You won't think that once you get to know her," Judi argued amicably. "There's not a person on this island who doesn't love her."

Nathan frowned, trying to make sense of the information. "I still don't like it!"

"Neither do I, but what choice do we have?"

Nathan signaled her to be silent with a squeeze of his hand on hers when he heard movement from behind. Tilly bustled into the room carrying a platter overflowing with carved roast beef, followed by Van Edwards juggling steaming bowls of mashed potatoes and green beans.

"Go ahead and get your drinks," Tilly directed to Nathan and Judi, pointing beyond the head of the table. "There's soda, iced tea, and a pitcher of ice water on the sideboard over there."

The older couple disappeared again into the kitchen. Judi looked tentatively at Nathan before rising from her seat.

"Iced tea for me," Judi said. "The caffeine might come in handy for what's ahead. What about you?"

Nathan puckered his brow. "Make it the same." It would take more than caffeine to make this evening bearable or palatable.

In a matter of minutes, everyone seated themselves around the table Tilly had completely loaded with food. Mr. Edwards gave a short, stiff prayer. When he finished, a tomblike silence engulfed the room. The quiet made Tilly scowl.

"Go on, now," she demanded. "Dig in before it gets cold. No sense in sulkin' when everything's gonna be all right."

Ever so slowly, the clinking of serving ware and dishes being passed filled the void, but tension remained high throughout the meal. The delicious down-home food seemed to be squandered on such a dour group, and Nathan knew this upset the matronly woman. Soon the meal drew to a close, and Mr. Edwards seemed ripe to start their previous discussion by suggesting the group retreat to the living room.

"Which one of you is going to tell me what's going on?" the old man asked when the four assembled, flopping himself down into the overstuffed chair, linking his fingers together across his slightly plump belly.

Nathan was about to speak when Judi put a restraining

hand on his arm. "I'm responsible for this mess. Let me tell it." She looked sadly at the couple. "All I ask is for you to keep an open mind and to be reasonable at any requests Nathan might make of you."

"I'll keep an open mind," Mr. Edwards retorted, "but that's all I'm promising."

❧

Judi fidgeted, bouncing one foot nervously. In a sense, she should be glad to let loose her haunting past. Maybe Mr. Edwards would be able to help—or not. She didn't have a handle on the man yet. He was too much of an enigma.

She began her story slowly, gaining speed and strength as she continued, relating the threatening notes and sparing nothing of her former life that gave the menacing letters their power. Nathan sat stiffly beside her on the couch, brooding and unhappy. Occasionally, they exchanged glances, and he would give a slight assuring nod of his head, bestowing on her the much-desired encouragement she needed to continue.

"So, as you can see," Judi concluded, "Nathan didn't know anything about my faked death until he arrived on the island to see for himself that I was alive and well." She threw a penitent glance at Nathan. "I falsely believed he was the culprit. I was wrong! Because of this, he's spent the last two years going through the horrific pain of losing a spouse and ironically came to personally know Christ through the experience. Now we're just trying to find our way by doing what God would have us do." She drew her chin up as she looked at the old man. "I know the trouble I face is tremendous, but Nathan is innocent and shouldn't be made to bear the brunt of my problems."

A silence covered the room, and she heard Nathan take a tired breath.

"What do you say about that, young man?" Mr. Edwards's large blue eyes nailed Nathan like an arrow, his docile tone indecipherable.

Nathan shot back a look under frowning brows. "I say she's been quite patient, more so than I would have been, and bared her soul truthfully to the two of you." His gaze hardened. "Now I would like to know your intentions."

The old man's lips thinned. "I already know she's been truthful. I'm asking what your position is on what she said about your role as it relates to her problems."

"What are you getting at?" Nathan asked.

Judi drew a frustrated breath. Why couldn't Mr. Edwards understand? "I've already told you Nathan didn't know anything about the letters or my faked death. He's innocent!"

Nathan shook his head. "I don't think that's what he's talking about."

"You're right, young man," Mr. Edwards sternly agreed. "It's not my intentions, but yours that concern me. You are still her husband. What do you plan to do about that?"

Judi could tell Nathan was growing weary and angry at this line of questioning. What was Mr. Edwards up to? From his tone, it was difficult to know if he was seeking to help or harm. Tilly seemed to be taking everything in, processing the information like a court reporter. All she needed was a stenotype machine.

"Let me tell you something," Nathan said, his voice dropping dangerously low, "Judi is still my wife, and I'm going to do everything in my power to help her—including walking all over you if need be. She's played fair with the two of you even though you've drawn her here possibly under false pretenses, bullied, threatened, and frightened her—much like the person who wrote those menacing notes." He leaned forward on the seat, taking a stance similar to those Judi recalled him using in the courtroom when he wanted to intimidate. "If you want to threaten her with the law, then you'll have to go through me first."

A brief and puzzling smile lit on the old man's lips. "Don't go spitting fire like a sea dragon," the old man strangely responded. "You'll wear yourself out. If you plan to fight this thing sensibly, you'll need to conserve your strength."

"What are you saying?" Nathan demanded.

Tilly finally came to life with a knowing grin. "He's saying you're gonna get some help."

Nathan looked unsure, but Judi knew Tilly was right. Help had arrived!

eleven

Nathan stared at the ceiling, drawing his arms up then under the satin-covered feather pillow. What a strange and bizarre day. It might take him weeks, if not months, to straighten out what had gone on at Tilly Storm's house. How Mr. Edwards went from a grumpy old codger to a multitasking thinking machine couldn't be explained. Before Nathan had known it, the man was writing down the names and numbers of people he wanted Nathan to contact—the last being an extremely well-known and definitely expensive criminal lawyer.

"Don't worry about the cost," the old man had told them. Don't worry about the cost? Nathan could only dream of making in a lifetime what this fellow lawyer probably grossed on just one client. How could he not think about the cost?

The whole thing was off the wall, and he knew Judi's observations had been right. Mr. Edwards was more than he made himself out to be—more than a busboy at the Dairy Barn and more than a church elder in a small, obscure church on Bay Island. He knew too many important people, including congressmen and federal agents. Why Mr. Edwards should be living incognito among the islanders was a question worthy of asking. Why play out his golden years wiping down tables and hauling leaky, soda-filled trash bags to the restaurant Dumpster? It just didn't make sense. Surely, if the man was a wealthy philanthropist or even some type of retired government agent, why reside in an everyone-knows-everybody's-business place like Bay Island?

The old man was full of advice, as well. Nathan was to return as planned to Pennsylvania in the morning and immediately contact the criminal attorney who would be awaiting his call. He was to say nothing of Judi or his trip to Bay Island to anyone else as he prepared to present his eminent domain bill to the house floor. Nathan would then make a return round-trip to the island the following Monday to collect Judi for an appointment with the attorney in Harrisburg. In the meantime, Mr. Edwards would *take care* of the writing analysis, which he insisted could not be performed correctly unless an FBI expert executed the examination. Nathan tried to explain he was already in contact with a detective who was a pioneer in the field. This news didn't even faze the man.

The white-haired man just went on looking again at the copy of the threatening letter Nathan carried with him, the note so close to the man's thick glasses Nathan wondered how he could read it. When Mr. Edwards asked rhetorically whether Nathan had left his fingerprints on the notes when he copied them, he and Judi merely blushed in reply.

Mr. Edwards seemed so sure about what to do. Nathan wasn't so convinced, his head still swimming with the possibilities and complications of the new plan.

Somehow, through all of the intricate scheduling, he would have to fend off questions from his family, friends—and Lindsey. That could prove to be difficult.

Judi, however, had quickly embraced the old man's plan and seemed encouraged with the news that he believed her case was a winnable one. Most of all, the couple hadn't openly judged her poor choices and insisted she was still a valuable and much-wanted resident of the island and the congregation at their little redbrick church.

The sanguine expression on Judi's face said it all. Knowing she was still loved and accepted by those on the island was more important to her than the legal outcome of her dilemma. Yet a thick cloud of sadness exuded from her features when their eyes met. He knew she was thinking about what was at stake—including their husband and wife relationship.

Was this relationship salvageable? Could their marriage withstand the strain? Could he really trust Judi knowing what he did about her propensity toward secrecy and mistrust? God could change people. He knew this firsthand. Yet a person had to be willing to hand their life over to Christ for this transformation to happen. Judi claimed to have totally given her life to God—and Nathan believed her. But what he really wanted to know was if she was absolutely committed to giving up her previous methods of problem solving to focus on God's plan—not her own.

Another consideration needled him. What if Judi's con game had also included her marriage to him? She'd admitted her former insatiable need to achieve a lifestyle where she wouldn't have to scratch and claw to be like everyone else. Did that include marrying a man who could financially acquire such a position on this ladder of success? Maybe love never entered the picture where she was concerned. If so, would she admit to such treachery and willingly release him from a loveless marriage? The thought made his chest tighten. The fact was, he didn't want to be released. He still loved her in spite of everything. The realization didn't give him any satisfaction; it made him feel weak and foolish. How could any self-respecting man settle for anything less than a spouse who could fully return his love?

At best, even if she truly loved him, several obstacles stood ready and willing to drown them. Neither of their families seemed the least bit flexible concerning their marriage—not three years ago, and he could safely assume the new turn of events would exacerbate the tension. Judi would wither in such an environment after experiencing the love and acceptance she knew on the island.

Would these factors doom them to become another in the

long line of couples joining the dismal ranks of the divorced?

I'm lying on this bed with a lot of questions and few answers. God, I'm in need of serious counsel where Judi is concerned. I'll live in a loveless marriage if that's what You want, but it's not what I want. Yet living without her seems just as unbearable. It's not how You planned it, I'm sure!

I know her honor should have been defended when my family often treated her with disrespect. I'll make that right! I'm pleading with You to bring back the love I thought Judi had for me. If this is not to be, then please take away the desire that's gnawing at me. I don't think I could stand the pain of losing her again. Give me the perseverance to see this thing through. Your honor is at stake, too, and I never want it to be said that I've dishonored You in any way. Help me to trust You. I can't do this alone.

He turned to glance at the bedside clock. Time was quickly gaining on midnight and he knew sleep would not come easily. He checked the alarm setting one more time. A confirming red dot glowed back at him. He couldn't afford to miss the morning plane, not when so much depended on timing—and a stellar performance on the house floor.

❧

As Judi stood in front of her bedroom mirror adjusting the collar of her blouse, she was only too conscious of the shadows and strained lines etched around her eyes. Even her mouth looked strained and tight. She smiled experimentally, but her reflection looked stiff and artificial. Tilly wouldn't be happy with her peaked appearance, either, when she came by the church office to take Judi to lunch. She was sure of that.

There was a reason for the droopy appearance. Despondency! Yes, that's what it was. Nathan's plane would be halfway to Harrisburg by now and already her heart felt empty without him. He had called earlier to say his transport had arrived on time and to see if she was holding up after their taxing evening at Tilly's. She was holding up well, actually, mostly because she had felt so protected by Nathan during Mr. Edwards's inquisition and because his actions almost made her believe there was some spark left of their love.

Over the phone, Nathan's voice resonated with husbandly concern, and when he paused for several seconds, she was so sure he had to be sensing the growing fire within her coming through the airwaves that he was on the verge of pouring out the words she desired to hear. She waited, willing for any expression of love to come.

The words never came.

Instead, he told her to take care while he was gone and that he would call her sometime the next day after finishing with the house session.

What had she really expected, anyway? A fairy-tale ending to a mixed-up Cinderella turned modern-day runaway bride story? Tilly and Mr. Edwards assured her the church would continue to love and welcome her. Those words meant more than their weight in gold. Yet she wanted Nathan's love and acceptance even more. She was afraid she might not gain either.

Deciding not to morbidly dwell on the unforeseeable, she quickly finished dressing. Breakfast consisted of nothing more than a few gulps of orange juice and one very burnt piece of toast on her way out the door.

The morning went quickly as she worked on the lengthy quarterly report. She was thankful when Tilly turned out to be the only visitor to the church office. Tilly, however, was wired, evidently happy to be put in action again, and immediately tried to usher Judi out the door.

"You're lookin' a mite peaked today," observed Tilly, situating her purse over her forearm as they walked into the parking lot. Judi gave her a mocking I-knew-you'd-say-that smile, which the woman chose to ignore. "The burden of this bad business can't be good on a body."

Judi couldn't have agreed more. "I'm just worried about Nathan, that's all."

"God'll take care of him. Ain't no use to carry on when you can't do anything but pray about it." Tilly flopped herself into the driver's seat of her beat-up two-seater cart. "Thought we might ride over to Bell's Market for a bite to eat. They're havin' a mighty good Thursday special on their fried bologna sandwiches in the deli today."

"Who can resist fried bologna?" Judi remarked with a laugh, not daring to mention the island delicacy was not on Tilly's heart-smart diet. She felt her spirits lift a little. Tilly must have known how difficult the day would be for Judi and offered—no, demanded—they have lunch.

When they'd arrived at the market and ordered the special, Tilly hustled them outside to the backless, sun-drenched blue bench positioned against the storefront window.

"We can situate ourselves right here on the liar's bench," Tilly chuckled, letting her purse drop onto the sidewalk and giving it a swift kick under the wooden seat with her bone-colored orthotic shoes. "Hoggin' up the bench should keep the community gossipin' down for a spell. Too much lollygagging and jawin' going on here, anyway."

Judi smiled as she sat down, knowing that Tilly had spent more than her fair share of time *jawin'* on this very same bench with her own lady friends. The store was a popular hangout for the older crowd in the warm months. Taking a deep breath of the island air, Judi let her glance skip along the tree-lined street. How she loved this island with its small, oddball shops and family-owned businesses. The colorful characters inhabiting the island, nosy as they might be, could be counted on in a pinch. They really cared about people— took care of their own. She would hate to lose this priceless companionship and solidarity that had become so ingrained in her life.

Yet she knew her life was about to drastically change. The possibility of prison even loomed on the horizon. Nathan would leave her for sure if that happened. Then she would be totally, irrevocably alone.

Tilly gave Judi's hand a maternal pat, evidently sensing her poignant mood. "Everything's gonna be all right, you hear? Van will help get matters under way right quick. He's given Nathan a heap of sound advice to get the two of you young'uns through this briar patch."

Judi remained silent for a moment and then turned to face the matronly woman. "Just who is Van Edwards?"

Tilly looked momentarily flustered. "Whatever do you mean? You know who he is!"

"I know who he *appears* to be," Judi answered. "But there's more to him than meets the eye, isn't there?"

The question seemed to befuddle the woman further. "That's just a bunch of foolishness now. I really don't know why such a notion should enter your head."

"Really?"

"Really!"

"He does seem sweet on you," Judi went on, deciding to try another tactic, and was pleasantly surprised to see the shocked expression lighting up Tilly's face. Judi laughed. "You're not the only observant body on the island."

Tilly smoothed her tightly pulled-back hair with a busy hand. "That's gibberish!"

"Oh, come on," Judi said with a laugh. "The man's not left your side since last summer when you had the heart attack. You're like Frick and Frack together, bread and butter, Lucy and Desi—"

"Now stop all this foolishness," demanded Tilly, playfully swatting at Judi. "Seems to me this here liar's bench is havin' a terrible effect on you. And I'd be much obliged if you'd stop speculatin' on such matters."

Judi was finding great enjoyment in turning the tables on Tilly but decided to have mercy on the woman. "I'll quit for now. It just seems proper for the one who's always playing Cupid to occasionally be the recipient."

"That's for the young folk," Tilly asserted with a firm nod.

The thought caused Judi to linger over the words for a moment. "Sometimes it doesn't work for the young folks, either."

Tilly must have heard the slight catch in Judi's voice. Her face softened. "Nathan will do right by you."

But I haven't done right by him, Judi's soul accused right back. It was true! How could she argue with this self-judgment? Nathan always chose the high road, the straight and narrow—the path to help the greatest amount of people. He had the right character to take on the world. Even now, she could recall a time when he would have done anything for her.

"Do you know what caught my attention the first time I met Nathan?" Judi asked contemplatively, her mind actively going back in time.

"What was that, girl?" Tilly was at full attention, her eyes bright with curiosity.

"I had come to interview for a job as a legal aide in the law firm where he worked, an interview he'd obviously been relegated to perform for the first time." A wry smile came across her lips. "He was so handsome—and nervous. He wouldn't crack a smile for anything throughout the entire meeting, cross-examining me like a witness on the stand instead of a potential employee. Then he kept fidgeting with his papers and constantly writing things down on a clipboard. I could hardly take my eyes off of him with that cute cleft in his chin. I'm sure it made him tenser, but I didn't care. Not when I knew right then and there that he was someone I had to know everything about, someone I'd been waiting for."

Judi shifted on the bench and laughed as she continued.

"Finally, when we'd finished, he asked if I would fax over my references. I decided it was time for the poor man to loosen up a little. You should have seen the expression on his face when I told him I'd gladly fax over the original if he would send it right back since it was my only copy."

Drawing her eyebrows together in bewilderment, it only took a moment for understanding to light Tilly's eyes. "Did you finally get the smile you'd been waiting for?"

Judi nodded, feeling the prick of tears dangerously close to the surface at the endearing memory. "He looked at me with this stunned expression at first and then, like a closed flower opening for the first time, he just let out this huge, uninhibited laugh. He didn't stop for the longest time, as if his happiness had been trapped inside for too long. It was hard not be caught up in the contagiousness of the moment. I was laughing right along with him." Staring at her hands, she clasped them tightly together. "It was then he told me he'd do anything for me—since I seemed to be the only one who could not only make him laugh, but also knew so much about operating office equipment. He hired me on the spot—without the references."

"That's a sweet story, Judi."

"And now he's still doing everything he can for me."

"That's what love does for you."

"Love?" Judi could feel her heart shrink at the word. "He's doing what's right because he's respectable. I had hoped, but I think the love is gone." She let a sigh build and slowly let it loose. "Our love has been steadily siphoned away by my distrust and deceit. I think it's too late."

"That's a bunch of hogwash, girl," Tilly replied, her voice firm.

"No," Judi argued, shaking her head despondently. "You weren't there. You didn't see the look in his eyes when I accused him of sending those vile letters and then told him about my past. The whole thing disgusted him."

"He said that?" Tilly demanded.

"He didn't have to."

"Seems to me you're buying a peck of trouble without even knowin' what's in the basket." Tilly wagged a finger at her. "Don't go assumin' anything. You listen to ol' Tilly. I know what I'm sayin'." Her intent eyes snapped forcefully. "I'm tellin' you that boy loves you—but he's scared. You're gonna have to fight, to let him know how much you still cherish and trust him. No man likes to be made a fool of. He just wants to be loved and respected."

"I do love and respect him!"

"Then you gotta show him!"

"I don't know how," Judi lamented. "There's so little time."

"Then it's a good thing you got ol' Tilly around to give you some pointers," the older woman said with a wide, toothy smile. "Anything worth anything in this ol' world is worth fightin' for."

Judi wanted to believe. Could she fight and win his love back? Another thought caused her to halt briefly. If she won the prize of his love, would she lose her precious Bay Island in the exchange? Only God knew. One thing she did know: As much as she loved her newfound life on the island, her heart could never be complete without Nathan.

She had to fight—and win.

❧

The small aircraft bumped leisurely to a stop along the short island airstrip, and Nathan closed his eyes, still thanking God for allowing him the chance to complete the house session and see his dream bill passed by a wide margin. Pieces were falling nicely into place, including his call to the attorney. Mr. Edwards had certainly pulled enough strings to set him wondering again about the old man's true identity.

He was sure Judi would be relieved to know such a

competent attorney was working on her behalf. They would fly back tomorrow, Tuesday, to Harrisburg and meet the attorney face-to-face. Nathan hoped Mr. Edwards had been able to secure the handwriting analysis he'd promised in time for the meeting.

The weekend had been difficult. He had managed to dodge his family—but not Lindsey. They'd had a terrible quarrel, with Lindsey accusing him of seeing another woman. Little did she know! Nathan's evasiveness only made it worse, yet he knew there was too much at stake to risk telling her the truth. It hurt to know what he was doing to her. He had no other choice.

Thomas, his legislative aide, had proved himself invaluable, seeing to every little detail at the statehouse. He'd offered his help, gone about his business, and kept Nathan's matters to himself. What more could Nathan ask for?

Nathan unclipped his lap belt and followed the pilot as he opened the door. Standing in the arch, he saw Judi waiting patiently by the small airport tower in her golf cart. She waved her arm in greeting. He waved back and stepped off the plane.

They had talked twice on the phone while he was away. She seemed different somehow, more confident perhaps, or just calmer knowing the statehouse session had gone well and the attorney was already working on her case. He, on the other hand, had become more restless. He shouldn't have given in to the urge to go through Judi's belongings at their house, or worse yet, spent hours intently going through their picture albums.

The deep emotions and pain he felt were inexplicable. It was like plodding through their courtship and marriage, again leading up to the big climax where she died—where the pictures suddenly stopped. The emotions tore through him once more, like watching a movie over and over, knowing the ending, yet the suspense leading to the conclusion still gripping terribly at the heart every time.

The occasion gave him time to reflect on their past as a couple. Yes, Judi had deceived him and maligned his integrity. At the same time, he'd dismissed her concerns and legitimate needs over his desire to achieve a lifelong goal of serving the people of Pennsylvania. Noble as his gesture might have been, he'd failed as a husband. He could see that now. How he had been so blind while taking the journey was still a mystery. A man of detail should never have missed the obvious signs of his own shortcomings.

"How was your flight?" Judi greeted when he finally reached the end of the tarmac. Her strawberry-red hair flipped lightly in the afternoon breeze and her rosy cheeks seemed kissed by sun. She looked relaxed behind the wheel.

He gave her a grin. "It was a beautiful day for flying," he answered, suddenly glad to be back on the island. "Have you been doing okay?"

"Much better now that you're back," she answered with a welcoming smile, her green eyes meeting his. "I'm glad you're here!"

He frowned, tossing his bag into the back of the cart. "Why? Is something wrong?"

"No," she said with a delicate shrug. "I just missed you, that's all."

Something in her eyes sent a spark along his chest and triggered his pulse to racing. The look reminded him so much of the photos he'd just seen when they'd first married, reviving yet another forgotten ember.

"Is that so hard to believe?" she went on as he slid into the passenger seat.

He turned easily toward her, resting his elbow on the seat between them. His gaze fell on her face and then her lips. Her slight smile was openly disarming.

"You're sure everything is all right?" he asked again, marveling at her composure. This was not the same woman he had left on the island.

Slowly, she leaned close. "I'll prove it," came her whispery-light response. One soft hand cupped the side of his face as she gently pressed her lips to his.

Her kiss momentarily stunned him, but when she began to withdraw, her green eyes openly questioning his reaction to her gesture, his arms quickly pulled her forward again, claiming her mouth with his. The feel of her mouth and breath caused an explosion of familiar longing within him, taking him back to the happier times they had enjoyed early in their marriage. Feeling her eager response filled him with joy—and fear—that she was once again, at that moment, completely his.

Slowly, he drew her back and they stared at each other. He searched her face for recognition or acknowledgment of what they had just shared. What he saw was a mirror of his own uncertainty mixed with a strong longing and desire to be one again.

Judi traced his chin with her finger and he turned to see if anyone was watching. It was ludicrous to be sitting in a golf cart in the middle of an airport kissing like passionate lovers. The islanders would think they were kissing cousins. Thankfully, there were only two lonely bystanders wandering around the small airport tower. He didn't know where his pilot had gone.

Judi dropped her hand. "Are you angry?" she asked, her voice husky and low.

He drew his gaze back to her. "No."

"You're embarrassed, then?" It was her turn to peruse the tower and airfield.

"Frankly," Nathan said, scratching at the back of his neck, his eyes roaming back with a will of their own to her lips again, "I'm not sure what I am." The intensity of his emotions scared him more than anything he'd encountered in the past week.

"Then I have to tell you something."

Nathan's heart sank. A bomb was going to land, he was sure of it. "What do you need to tell me?" he asked, bracing for the worst.

"I love you, Nathan Whithorne!"

twelve

Judi refused to turn her gaze away as she tried to capture the various emotions stirring across Nathan's face. She had just bared her soul, open and unprotected, laying everything she had on the line with three little words. It was a risky business. He had just returned from home, and although it pained her to think about it, Nathan had most certainly spent some time with the woman he'd previously pledged to marry—another who claimed to love him. Which way would Nathan eventually turn? Was his heart torn between the two women? Right now, she was his wife and decidedly had the edge, but eventually one would be the winner and the other the loser. Surely the love they had shared in the past counted for something and the way he'd just kissed her revealed he wasn't totally devoid of feelings for her.

"Well," she finally asked in frustration, watching him rub the back of his neck in contemplation, "aren't you going to say something?"

His hand dropped and he lifted one eyebrow. "Wow!"

"Wow?" Judi frowned. Was that all the man could say? Kissing Nathan had produced more than a *wow* for her— much more. It had awakened every fiber of her consciousness to the love she knew was ready to let loose. It had been suppressed and held dormant for so long, it could no longer be held against its will. If Nathan rejected her—if God chose this to be—she would resign herself to live with this one-sided love, a strong bond she would never fully realize.

But she hadn't lost the battle yet. The fight had just begun, and she didn't plan to give up easily. With determination,

Judi started the ignition.

Nathan immediately grasped her hand, his features impossible to interpret. "Now you're angry."

"No," she answered, turning back toward him, feeling the warmth of his hand. "There's no anger. Matter of fact, I can't tell you how good it is to have you back on the island." She returned his stare, captivated by the intensity of his exquisite gray eyes. "But we do have to get back to the business at hand. Mr. Edwards received the handwriting analysis this morning and wanted me to bring you to Tilly's as soon as you arrived."

His eyes immediately narrowed in interest. "Did he say anything about the results?"

"No," she said with a shake of her head. "He just seemed anxious for me to get you there."

"Then I suppose we should do as he asked." Nathan dropped his grip on her hand and settled back into the seat, his eyes momentarily closed.

Judi turned the cart around and started down the long drive next to the runway. She gave him a quick sideways glance. "I turned in my resignation today."

His eyes snapped open, and he seemed to study her a moment before speaking. "Are you sure that was wise?"

"What else could I do?" she asked, stopping at the end of the road and then turning right. "We'll be leaving in the morning to see the attorney, and I can't leave the church in a bind if I'm not able to come back." She slowed down to make another turn. "I've already secured a temporary replacement for the next two weeks. After that—I guess they'll have to hire someone."

Nathan didn't comment but quietly kept his gaze on the road ahead while looking deep in thought. Judi didn't want to make too much of his comment about her resignation, but she had to wonder at the surprise, or perhaps it was disappointment, in his voice. Surely he knew for her to remain on the island two things would have to happen—exoneration from all criminal charges and the church's willingness to let her continue in their employ. Did Nathan believe she was going to come out on top of this legal tangle? Was he already planning for her possible return to the island— alone? She didn't hold much hope of him leaving his beloved Pennsylvania. A terrible thought struck. Maybe he had already made his choice. That might explain his mixed reaction to her kiss and verbal declaration of love.

Judi stopped the cart to let a laughing group of tourists cross at the next intersection, instinctively waving back at their friendly gestures. She smiled. Like her, the strangers seemed to be under the island's spell, and she felt a responsive bond with the affable visitors. The island was her sanctuary, a calming hideaway from the rest of the world.

"Is the island always this busy during the weekdays?" Nathan asked as they moved forward again.

Judi turned and gave him a brief look. "From Memorial Day until Labor Day. The weekends stay full until the end of October."

Nathan nodded and fell silent again until they reached Tilly's cabin. When Judi cut the ignition and slipped off her seat belt, he gripped her arm lightly, and she looked at him expectantly.

"Mr. Edwards has secured one of the best lawyers money can buy," Nathan remarked, looking quite serious. "But I think we should still be careful around the man until we know more about his real interest. He could be a humanitarian who goes about helping people in need, or he could be something more. As a public representative, I need to be careful."

"You think he might be a political saboteur?" she asked, trying to picture the opinionated old man working for one of Nathan's opponents. The vision was too ridiculous for words. Although their approaches were vastly different, Mr. Edwards and Nathan held a duplicate likeness when it came to being a straight arrow. No, the two of them were working on the same side. "I don't believe you have anything to worry about, Nathan; but I'll be careful all the same."

Nathan nodded and led them onto the porch deck where he rapped on the door. Tilly came to greet them looking unusually solemn, and Judi immediately felt on the alert. Nathan's taut expression let her know he'd sensed the change, too.

"Come on in, you two," Tilly said, ushering them inside.

Mr. Edwards stood stiffly behind the living room chair. "Have a seat," he directed when the two entered the room.

"Think I'll stand, if you don't mind," Nathan returned, and Judi tensed when he passed on the niceties. "You have the results of the analysis?"

The old man nodded grimly. "It found a credible match."

The room turned stone cold and silent. Judi felt her heart slam against her ribs, pounding like a hammer. It couldn't be true!

"That's impossible," Judi blurted, breaking the unnerving void. She shook her head. "I don't care what the test says; it must be wrong. Nathan did not write those letters."

"I didn't say it matched with him," the old man asserted, staring at Judi with his magnified blue eyes. "The test cleared Representative Whithorne."

Nathan looked as stunned and confused as she felt. "I don't understand."

Mr. Edwards and Tilly didn't speak right away, but both continued to look at Judi with a mixture of pity, uneasiness, and regret.

"What?" Judi demanded. Slowly it all registered in her tired brain. "You think I wrote the notes?" Disbelief sent shock waves through her numb body. "That's crazy!"

Immediately Nathan sent her a cautionary glance and slowly turned to the old man. "Exactly what did the test reveal? You weren't given a sample of Judi's handwriting."

"Will the two of you stop conjecturing and just sit down so I can tell you what the test did say?" Mr. Edwards barked, firmly sitting down in the chair, obviously expecting everyone else to follow suit.

Tilly quickly swished over and lowered herself in the chair beside Mr. Edwards. Judi heard Nathan sigh and felt his hand on her back as he led her to the couch where he indicated for her to sit. He dropped inaudibly down beside her.

"Please continue." There was palpable constraint in Nathan's voice.

"That's better," the old man responded. "Let's get something straight. The writing didn't match Nathan, and as he just mentioned, we didn't have a sample for Judi. It was neither of you."

"Then who?" Judi murmured, totally mystified.

"It was the person who endorsed one of the checks Mr. Whithorne gave me to analyze," answered the white-haired man, his piercing eyes zeroing in on Judi. "It was a man by the name of Stanley Porter!"

"There's no way!" Judi felt unwell. A sick feeling at the pit of her stomach burned like fire, and her stricken lungs needed air. "My father?"

&

"It just doesn't make sense," Judi said, wiping her nose again. In her shock she hadn't cried at Tilly's place last night, but she'd let loose once she'd arrived at the condo. Now she was on a commuter flight with Nathan, and the tears were on the verge of coming again.

Nathan squeezed her hand. "I can't explain it, either."

"Your campaign manager would have made a better suspect than my father," she contended with a sniffle. "I didn't even know you'd given him money. He had never said a word about it."

Nathan shrugged. "He seemed low on funds after his last hospitalization. I was only trying to help, but he wasn't very receptive."

"Why has it been so hard for our families to accept us?" Judi balled up the tissue in one hand. "Why couldn't they just be happy for us?"

"Maybe we should have given them more time to warm up to the idea and had a proper church wedding," speculated Nathan. "Eloping solved our problems but not theirs."

"How could something so trivial cause a father to hate his child enough to threaten her life? Some of those letters were so vile." She looked at Nathan, unshed tears blurring her vision. "I suppose he did have opportunity. He knew all about my past and could have taken my juvenile rehab identification badge." She shook her head in disbelief. "To think I went to such great lengths to make my plan work to protect him. I thought he was in danger."

"You need to listen to me, Judi," Nathan insisted, gently tipping her face toward him with his hand. "I don't know why your father sent those terrible letters, but you need to let go of it for the next few hours and save your energy for the attorney's visit this afternoon. We need to concentrate on getting you through the legal difficulties first." His thumb traced the line of her jaw. "I promise we'll get to the bottom of this."

Judi nodded and yielded to his touch when he soothingly brought her forward to lean on his chest. The comforting, even beat of his heart resounded against her ear, and she could feel the softness of his shirt, smell the scent of his familiar aftershave. Experiencing his protective arms around her shoulders calmed the wild beating of her own heart. With Nathan on her side she could almost believe the nightmare would work out into a manageable dream.

God. . .I didn't see this last development coming. My own father!

Am I to lose my family, too? I don't think I can bear it. Now, more than ever, I need to keep the husband You gave back to me. It feels so good to have his arms around me, to hear his steady breathing. I don't want to ever move from his hold. Please give Nathan the desire to keep our marriage together. What a joy it would be to serve You together. We'd make a great team! Change my heart to be what You desire, to make this thing work, even if it means forgiving those who have wronged us.

Judi snuggled further into his embrace, letting her heavy eyelids close and carry her tired body to a place of rest.

❧

"Come on and wake up, sleepyhead." Nathan gently shook Judi's shoulders and she stirred. He removed his anesthetized arm from behind her back, experimentally stretching his fingers to regain some circulation. "We've landed."

Judi's eyes fluttered open and she stared blankly at him for a moment. "We're here?" She let a yawn break free and immediately covered her mouth with her hand. "Sorry."

He gave a smile, glad to see her features more rested. Mr. Edwards's bolt from the blue the night before had taken a toll on both of them. They had to remain strong for what lay ahead. Quietly, he ushered Judi from the plane and to the airport parking lot.

"What a beautiful car," admired Judi when they reached the metallic blue sedan. She settled into the bucket seat, letting her hand slide over the expensive leather. "Isn't this the European car reputed to go from zero to sixty in fifteen seconds?"

"Actually it's seven seconds!" Nathan nodded appreciatively. "And it handles better than any car I've ever driven." He threw her a grin. "Although I must say, I'm growing quite fond of your golf cart. I might be hard put to choose between the two."

"I don't know," she said, cracking a small smile. "I'm willing to trade with you for a while."

"Perhaps I'll take you up on that offer." Nathan maneuvered into the heavy traffic and onto the freeway. Judi seemed lost in thought, looking out the window as if seeing civilization for the first time. The companionable silence let Nathan think through his plans for the next few days.

Thirty minutes later he pulled into a space in the law office parking lot and shut the engine off. "Ready?"

Nodding solemnly, Judi slipped out of the car and looked up at the tall building. Quietly they walked into the office and waited while the secretary looked at the scheduling sheet.

"Mr. Winslow is waiting for you," she announced, ushering them directly into the plush office.

As soon as the polished wood doors opened, Nathan caught sight of the huge plate glass window. But it was the enormous desk with a distinguished-looking man seated behind it that commanded the room's attention.

The man instantly looked up and smiled. "Ah, you've made it. Come on in and make yourselves comfortable." He stood to his feet, and Nathan could see that he was rather short and stocky. The middle-aged man firmly shook Nathan's hand and immediately turned his gaze to Judi. "And you must be Judi Whithorne. Nice to meet you."

Judi timidly took the offered hand. "Thank you for taking my case."

"A very interesting set of circumstances, I must say," Mr. Winslow noted warmly. "But I think you'll be happy with the news today."

Nathan liked the man; his warm, professional demeanor gave a welcoming feeling of interest and loyalty. "Then I take it you've had time to look over the information I gave you last week?" Nathan asked.

The attorney nodded and turned to Judi. "From what Representative Whithorne has told me, you had obtained the birth certificate of a child who had died and with this document you made a new identity, subsequently obtaining driver's licenses in Pennsylvania and Ohio as this new person. You then faked a drowning death and have been living on Bay Island, Ohio, since that time. Does that sound correct?"

"Yes!" Judi looked nervously reserved.

"Let's deal with the licensing issue first." Mr. Winslow slowly swiveled back and forth in his chair. "The most either state could do for falsification is charge you with a misdemeanor, slap you with a fine, and put you in jail for six months if they felt so inclined."

Judi tensed and Nathan placed his hand reassuringly on her arm. "But you have good news about that, right?"

The lawyer gave a reassuring smile. "The fact that you came forward of your own accord has worked in your favor across the board. To be honest, neither state has a desire to waste their time on a misdemeanor case where there's been no intent to perpetrate a major crime. They are struggling enough trying to track down illegal immigrants and check scammers. It would be hard to justify spending several thousand dollars to collect a one-thousand-dollar fine or to make an example of you. So we're going to destroy both driver's licenses and the birth certificate and pay the fines."

Judi leaned forward, gnawing at her bottom lip. "But I also have a Social Security card."

"Not a big deal," Winslow asserted with confidence, chuckling at Judi's look of disbelief. "Although it goes against the grain of the American justice system, the feds aren't terribly interested in you, either." He scratched at the side of his nose. "The Social Security number will be revoked, of course, but the worst that will happen is that all the monies you paid into the system using that number will be lost. If you had tried to withdraw money from the program, that would be another story, but without any theft, and because of the circumstances that caused you to falsify your identification, they don't care to prosecute."

"That is great news!" Nathan's confidence in the man was growing. Right now he was thankful Mr. Edwards had steered them in the right direction.

"I believe," Winslow continued, tilting his head in thought, "I can get you through this entire process without any criminal charges being filed."

"None?" Judi perked up. "How can that be?"

"It can be done, but it will be cost some money."

Nathan knew this was coming. "How much?"

"Your biggest outlay will be in restitution to the city and county," he said matter-of-factly.

"Restitution?" Judi asked.

"The city and county will want to be reimbursed for the rescue and recovery attempts they made. It won't be cheap!" Winslow began ticking off items on his fingers. "There will be the police department's man hours, canine units, dive teams, and the detective's investigation to recoup—to the tune of around fifty thousand dollars."

"Fifty thousand dollars!" There was awe in Judi's voice.

"And if we make restitution," Nathan asked, still sorting through the details, "then the city and county prosecutors won't press charges, is that right?"

"They'll probably kiss your ring for saving them the time and expense of attempting to prosecute such a case." He shrugged his bulky shoulders. "If you don't or can't pay back this money, or if they decided to formally charge Judi, there's a good chance I could still get a jury acquittal. Realize, however, there are some risks and there will still be court fees and possibly fines to pay. Another possibility if you were charged would be for you to agree to plead guilty to lesser charges and make restitution, which brings us back to where we started."

"Then we'll pay the city and county up front!" Nathan

looked determinedly at Judi and then at the attorney. "There's no sense in taking a chance."

"I have absolutely no money, Nathan," protested Judi. "Where would we be able to scrape up that kind of money?"

"Let's not worry about that now!" Nathan would find the money, even if it meant selling their house. He turned back to Winslow. "What else?"

"There's the matter of the life insurance policy." Winslow tilted his head toward Nathan. "From what you've said, twenty-five thousand was donated to a charity. Unfortunately, the insurance company could not care less where the money went—they'll just want it back immediately."

"That's over seventy-five thousand, so far," Judi needlessly pointed out.

"The last matter will take more time than money to fix." The lawyer leaned back in his chair as he looked at Judi. "A judge has declared you to be legally dead. We have to get that reversed and revive your real Social Security number. Until those steps are done, you won't be able to hold a job or apply for a driver's license—anything that requires identification or a background check."

"How much time do you think that will take?" Nathan asked.

He shrugged again. "It might take weeks, but I'll do my best to speed the process along."

"Anything else?" Nathan was roughly calculating what it would take to pay the debts.

"I think we've discussed all the major issues."

"Except for your fees," Nathan added.

A surprised look crossed Winslow's face. "My fees? They're already covered."

"Covered?"

"An anonymous donor is paying my fees," he answered. "I thought you knew that."

Nathan looked at Judi, who returned a suspicious nod. "Mr. Edwards?"

"I really can't say," he said with a knowing smile. "All I can tell you is that my services have already been taken care of, and I'll do the best job I can." His smile slowly faded. "I understand that you have recently discovered the identity of the author of the threatening notes. If you need my help in that matter, I'll represent you." He looked at Judi. "Do you have any plans to file charges?"

The stricken look on her face answered the question. "No matter what my father has done, I can't do that to him."

The attorney nodded with understanding. "Unfortunately, I can't solve or heal family problems like the one you're facing." He leaned forward, his elbows on the desk. "Are there any other questions I can answer for either of you?"

"No," Nathan answered. "You've been very helpful. I'll let you know when the money is secured to make restitution."

"Very well," concluded Winslow. "My secretary has some papers for you to sign and then you're free to go. Will you be staying here or going back to the island?"

Nathan felt Judi's gaze on him. "We have some family business to take care of before we make any career or relocation plans."

"Another set of decisions I can't help you with." There was empathy in the attorney's eyes.

"I know!" Nathan stated.

Only God can!

thirteen

Judi stood alone in the master bedroom slowly turning in a circle to take in the surroundings. The memorable sights and smells belonging to her previous life were coming alive and rushing at her with thrusters on full burn, penetrating her soul with unbearable longing. It was as if she was returning to the pages of a suspenseful but unfinished novel she laid aside years ago. With a heavy sigh, she sank onto the king-size bed and absently smoothed out a crease along the wedding ring quilt.

Like a fog lifting, she could feel her heart respond to the surroundings. She had purposely closed away these pictures of her past and now they were being dusted off and put back into service.

She wished Nathan was with her at this moment; but in the silence of their house, she was quite alone.

Instead, Nathan was with Lindsey, explaining what he couldn't convey in a phone conversation. He hadn't volunteered any insight into what he was going to say to the woman, and Judi had been too afraid to ask. With a sense of foreboding, she watched him back out of the driveway and speed off toward the west end of town. It was hard not to worry about the outcome of his visit with this woman who also claimed to love him, but Judi had to preserve her physical and emotional energy to focus on what was scheduled next—her father. It was a visit she dreaded but desperately needed in order to understand why her father would have done such a thing.

How was she going to get through this meeting with her

father when she'd been a total basket case just listening to Nathan's phone conversation with him? There had evidently been some hesitancy at her father's end of the line when Nathan explained his urgent need to see him, but Nathan had been firm and the older man eventually agreed to meet.

If that weren't enough, Nathan's entire family would be gathering at the house in less than four hours. Although she understood the necessity for the announcement of her return to be quick and efficiently executed, the sheer weight of the project besieged her. Nathan had warned that the media would be onto them within twenty-four hours and they needed to reach their family members before it had a chance to blow up. He had already been in contact with the statehouse, though she didn't know the particulars. Nathan wouldn't discuss it—not yet.

Judi took a deep breath and blew it out between pursed lips. Her gaze landed on the jewelry box sitting cockeyed on the dresser—her jewelry box. Getting up, she made her way across the room and carefully lifted the lid. Several glittering gems sparkled in the light. Piece by piece she examined the necklaces and rings, tilting her favorite opal ring to see the brilliant fire of color. Slowly she placed the ring back in the holder and continued her search. Her grandmother's ruby brooch was glaringly absent.

It was then she saw another ring—a gold band.

Nathan's wedding ring.

Carefully she lifted the ring and held it between her fingers. The beaded edge was slightly worn and Judi smiled sadly. The jeweler had explained that over the years the edging of their matching rings would eventually wear down into a radiant, shiny gold—a tribute to a long and happy marriage, the man had said.

Judi wondered how long Nathan had worn the ring before

taking it off for the final time and placing it in the dormant jewelry box. What went through his mind when the decision came? Lost in thought, she stared at the gold band.

There was a slight sound from behind and suddenly she knew she was no longer alone. Slowly she turned to see Nathan leaning against the doorjamb watching her, his face solemn. For a long moment neither spoke.

"I thought you might be in here," he finally said, breaking the spell of the silence. His tired eyes pivoted to the ring she held then back to her. He gently pushed off from the door frame and came near. "My wedding band."

Judi nodded, instantly feeling intrusive. "I'll put it back."

His hand shot out and captured hers. "I don't want it back in the box."

Confused, but hopeful, she looked up to meet his captivating gaze. The expression on his face made mincemeat of her insides. He was fighting against the same stresses threatening to take her under and yet there was vivid fire in his eyes. With awareness he took the ring from her hand and slid it over his finger.

"This past week has thrown my entire world into a vortex of chaos." Nathan's voice was low and expressive. "So many choices and possible directions to go." He gave a slight shake of his head. "I had no idea what I was going to say to handle Lindsey today, and I asked God to show me how to make an impossible situation a possible thing for Him."

"And what did He show you?" Her breath felt suspended as her chest ached for the answer.

"That I have already committed to love and cherish the woman I married." Nathan gently took her face between his hands. "We said it would be for better or for worse. We're experiencing the 'worse' part now, and I'm willing to hold out for the 'better' portion to come." He sighed. "I've not always been the best husband. I know that!"

"It's not true," Judi cried, clasping her hands over his. "I'm the one to blame. It was immature of me to be jealous of your political work. I should have trusted you enough to know your long hours of work weren't a reflection that you loved your job more than me—or that you weren't trying to get rid of me. If only I had come to you. I'm so sorry!"

Nathan leaned closer. "We've both made mistakes in the past, but we have to look to the future. We have something very solid to bond us together that was missing before."

"God!"

"Are you willing to see if God can bring us together as one again?"

"Willing?" she cried, drawing one hand endearingly down his chin. "I've been desperately praying for it."

Nathan imprisoned her hand and pulled her close, his lips beginning an exploration of her face, kissing her cheeks, chin, and eyes, moving into the hollow of her neck. "I've missed you so much. When you disappeared—"

The obvious pain in his voice tore at her heart, and she gently put her fingers to his lips and hushed him. "I'm here now and I promise to stay this time." Judi felt a great surge of happiness when he kissed her again.

Slowly he pulled her back. "I wish we didn't have to deal with our families this afternoon."

Judi sagged against his chest feeling the tightening of his grasp. "I can do anything as long as you're beside me, Nathan."

"I love you, Judith!"

Closing her eyes, she reveled in the depth of his tone, the beauty of his words. For several minutes they stayed in the close embrace, Judi never wanting to leave the warmth of his touch.

Suddenly, she heard a gasp from the doorway and both jerked toward the sound. Nathan's sister stood in the doorway, her mouth gaping in utter surprise.

"Judi?"

❧

"Are you sure Laurie's going to be all right by herself?" Judi asked when they pulled out of the driveway. "She looked absolutely floored."

Nathan sent her a sideways glance. "She'll be okay! I never thought she might make it into town this early and use the spare key. That was my fault." He looked in the side-view mirror before changing lanes. "I'm sure my cryptic message insisting that she meet at the house tonight with the rest of the family sent her into a panic."

"She won't tell the rest of your family before tonight, will she?" Judi looked at him doubtfully.

"She promised not to, but one can never tell."

Remembering the shocked expression on Laurie's face sent shivers through Judi. If Laurie had reacted with such alarm, Judi could only imagine how her own father was going to respond. Her hands were beginning to sweat as they drew closer, finally turning into her father's driveway.

Nathan turned to her. "Stay in the car until I give you the signal. We don't want to give him a heart attack. Let me talk with him first."

Mutely, she nodded and once again sent up a prayer for guidance. Nathan got out of the car and walked onto the porch stoop and rapped on the door. She saw the front door open and a second later Nathan disappeared inside. Nervously, she clenched her hands together, feeling the tremors of apprehension coursing through them. Her emotions were seesawing with joy from Nathan's affirmation of love and God's mercy to exonerate her from criminal litigation, to despair over her father's behavior—and over seventy-five thousand dollars in debts she had no idea how to pay.

Suddenly Nathan appeared at the front door, beckoning her to come. As she opened the car door, she caught a glimpse of her father trying to see around Nathan. When she reached the front steps and then the door, she heard his surprised intake of breath.

"It can't be true," her father sputtered as he hurriedly skirted around Nathan and embraced her with a fierce hug that threatened to break her ribs. He pulled her back to look into her face. "It's you. It's really you!" Once again, he held her close, and she felt him shudder, a sob reverberating against her shoulder.

"I've missed you, Daddy," she exclaimed, tears forming in her eyes as she looked questioningly at Nathan. The old man seemed genuinely overcome with elation at her return. How could he be the one who'd sent her such hateful letters? "Can we talk, Daddy?"

Reluctantly, her father released his hold and stepped back, wiping his face against the sleeve of his worn shirt. His thinning gray hair looked unkempt and wild, a scraggly three-day beard prickled over his jowls.

"Let me straighten up a little so we'll have a place to sit," her father said, immediately setting about to clear strewn newspapers from the couch. He dumped the papers behind a chair and turned to the couple, thrusting out an anxious hand indicating for them to sit. "When Nathan told me you were alive, I just couldn't believe it. I'm not sure I can believe it now even though I see you." He dropped into a chair and shook his head as if to clear his mind. "What happened to you? Where have you been all this time?"

Judi sat on the edge of the sagging couch within easy reach of her father. "I've been living on an island off Lake Erie for the past two years. The drowning accident never happened. It was all a fake."

Stanley Porter cradled his forehead with one hand. "A fake? But why?" Then he turned to Nathan. "You knew about this?"

"Listen to me, Daddy," Judi intervened, touching her father's knee. "Nathan didn't know anything about it until last week." She waited until her father looked at her again. "I left because someone was sending me threatening notes. I feared for my safety and yours." Contritely she gave Nathan a look. "I mistakenly thought Nathan had sent them. I was wrong!"

"You faked your own death because of those letters?" The old man's face paled. "That can't be!"

Judi pressed on, her heart thumping wildly. "Did you write those letters?"

"Me!" A haunted look pierced his eyes.

"I need to know the truth."

The old man seemed winded, his eyes darting riotously. "It wasn't supposed to turn out like this."

"Like what?"

"You were supposed to come back home to me," he blurted breathlessly, "not kill yourself."

Judi looked at Nathan, who shrugged his shoulders and nodded for her to keep talking. "I don't understand. Why was I supposed to come home?"

There was agony on the man's face. "Don't you see? Nathan didn't love you, and his family was killing your spirit day by day with their uppity snobbery. I could see how unhappy you were."

"But the letters were so. . .hurtful." Judi had to pause a moment to gain control of her voice. "How were those awful notes going to help me be happy?"

"By coming home where you belong!" her father answered, one shaky hand resting on his knee. "I wanted you to come to me for help, but when you didn't come, I figured you might have gone to Nathan about the notes. That just wouldn't do. He didn't care about you. He only cared about making money and being a famous politician." He looked accusingly at Nathan. "You know it's true!"

Judi closed her eyes for a second. "Oh, Daddy!"

"Don't you see? I had to change tactics. That's when I stuffed the chimney flue with a bird's nest after sending you the letter about the carbon monoxide. I thought for sure if you believed Nathan was trying to harm me, you'd have to come to me then." His voice cracked. "But you died instead! I assumed you'd been so distraught that you committed suicide."

"Is that why you've treated Nathan so badly?" Judi asked. "You thought he was ultimately responsible for making those threatening letters necessary? That was wrong, Daddy, no matter what your reasons were."

The old man nodded. "He's no good for you, Judi."

"Daddy, he's the man I love." Her voice was gaining strength. "You shouldn't have tried to come between Nathan and me. We would have worked it out."

Nathan rested a comforting hand on Judi's back and began to speak. "Sir, I do take partial responsibility. You were right about the fact that I should have been a better husband and not let my family treat her with disrespect. I plan to change all that." He stared back at her father's wide-eyed expression. "We can't alter what's already happened. We can only move forward. In light of that, Judi and I have agreed that it would be of no use for anyone else to know that you wrote those notes. We would like to clear the slate."

"He's right, Daddy," Judi chimed in. "We want you to be

part of our lives." She grew serious. "But you have to promise not to interfere with our marriage again. That's between Nathan and me."

"But what are you going to do now?" her father asked, consternation on his face.

"I don't know!" Judi answered truthfully.

Stanley looked at Nathan. "You don't have any plans?"

"We have a lot of details to work out with our attorney, families, and my career," Nathan told him. "My first priority, however, is to protect Judi, and I'll do what it takes to accomplish that. In the meantime, we're going to go wherever God leads us."

"God?" The word sounded foreign on her father's lips.

For the next few minutes, Judi expressed how God had miraculously changed their lives. "God can help you as much as He's helped us. You need Him."

The old man shook his head. "I don't have time for no religion."

"I'm not talking about religion, Daddy," she said with a rueful smile. "I'm talking about a personal relationship with Christ."

Her father took a deep breath. "Another time, Judi."

Nathan cautioned her with a nod. "I think he's been through enough for one day. He's still in shock by your appearance." He looked at his watch. "And we need to get back to the house before my family comes."

"You'll be coming back, right?" There was alarm in her father's voice.

Judi stood and gave him a big hug. "I'm not going anywhere. I already promised Nathan I'd never run off again."

It was a promise she planned to keep!

❧

Nathan rounded the street corner and spotted three cars in

the driveway. That could only mean Laurie had spilled the beans and the family was already gathered. Great! Just great! The day had been extremely draining, and he wondered if he would be able to keep pace on the last leg of the relay.

The visit with Lindsey had taken a toll on him. She had gone from being devastated and angry one minute to cajoling and pleading the very next. Just when she seemed accepting of the inevitable, she would beg him to reconsider what he was doing. Nathan was torn by her grief, but no amount of pain could keep him from making the decision he knew God wanted—the one he himself desired. Judi's response to him confirmed he had made the right choice.

"Nathan, your family is already here," Judi said with dismay.

"I know." Nathan parked the car behind his parents' luxury sedan and shut off the engine. He saw the living room curtains move and felt several pairs of eyes on them. "Laurie never could keep a secret."

"I was hoping to have time to talk with you before meeting them," Judi remarked jadedly, clutching her purse.

"I know! There's so much we have to discuss."

"Before we go in, I want to show you something." Judi rummaged around inside her purse and brought out a velvet bag. Tipping it up, a glimmering diamond ring and band spilled into her hands.

Nathan looked at the jewelry. "Your wedding rings."

"I brought them with me, hoping. . ." The color heightened in her cheeks. "I thought maybe, if you didn't mind, I'd like to wear them again."

Taking the rings from her trembling hand, he placed them on her finger. "I was hoping you still had them." He gently kissed her, feeling the warmth of her lips. She tasted so sweet.

The sound of the front door opening caused him to sit back with a sigh of exhaustion and look over at his parents standing impatiently in the doorway. He unsnapped his seat belt.

"Be brave," he instructed, squeezing Judi's hands.

Utter chaos reigned for the first five minutes when they entered the house. Questions began flying back and forth until Nathan's head ached.

"Quiet!" The loud reverberation of his voice instantly had an effect and a hush settled over the room. "I can't answer twenty questions at one time. I've already explained that Judi's drowning did not happen, and I've told you about the threatening letters that caused this whole chain of events."

"Have you seen these notes?" his normally soft-spoken father asked, throwing a suspicious glance Judi's way. "You say she knows who wrote the letters, but you won't tell us. How do you know these letters even existed?"

Nathan gave his father a stern look, a rush of anger coming over him at his father's tone. "Yes, I have seen the notes, and yes, I know who wrote them. It will serve no purpose for you to know the identity of this person."

"But—" His mother began to interrupt, holding up her delicate hand.

"Let's get something straight." Nathan's voice grew harsh as he looked from face to face. "Judi has been treated shamefully by this family, and I will not let it happen again. It's time I stood up and acted like the man of this house. Maybe we were wrong to go off and get married without anyone knowing, but that doesn't give anyone in this room the right to bully or slight her. She is my wife, and we come as a package deal. You'll treat her as you treat me."

Nathan's mother drew a delicate handkerchief to her mouth. "But we've always treated her well."

"Please don't deny what I already know." Nathan's features refused to soften as they usually did when addressing his mother. "Everyone in this room has been disrespectful to Judi in one way or another. Again, I want you to know I love Judi and we are still a married couple."

"But what about Lindsey?" asked Laurie, a worried expression intensifying across her brow.

"I've already explained the state of affairs to Lindsey and although it's been an unfortunate situation for her, she will come through this."

Once again questions began. Nathan fielded each subject as best he could, explaining the complexities of the circumstances.

"What about your elected seat in the statehouse?" his father asked, still giving sour looks to Judi. "You can't just give it up."

"I already have!" Nathan heard Judi's quick intake of breath, and he ruefully turned to her. "I'm sorry. I had hoped to discuss this with you before the family arrived." Judi's quick smile of understanding gave him courage to continue. "Although it is possible for me to retain the seat, it would mean a media circus that would inevitably hurt all of us and work against my fellow lawmakers."

"You're throwing away all your hard work," his father charged, the color deepening across his already ruddy face. "All you have to do is tell them Judi suffered from amnesia and recently got her memory back. It might even gain you points."

"Maybe it would," Nathan responded. "But spinning the story won't gain points with God. There will be no lies or deception. The people I serve have supported me because I gave them what they wanted—honesty and a genuine interest to see our state grow. Lies have no gain."

"Honesty has its place, son," his father continued. "But you're going to lose everything, and I don't think you're going to like living on the other side of the money belt."

Nathan smiled. "I'm not trying to build an empire. It's more important to lay my treasure with God where it belongs. The book of Matthew tells us to seek God's kingdom first." He looked at those gathered in the room. "No, I can't say that I want to live in poverty, but if I don't like it here, I'm certainly not going to like living like a pauper when I reach heaven because I have nothing to show for my life."

Jeff stood and shook Nathan's hand. "I'll support you, brother, in whatever you do. And if you need help searching online for a job, I'm your man."

Nathan smiled and gripped his brother's shoulder. "I appreciate that." He turned to Judi. "But I already have a job, if Judi is agreeable." There was uncertainty written across her face, and he gave her a reassuring grin. "I've been offered a partnership in a law firm in Cleveland with a new branch office on Bay Island."

"Nathan, when did this happen?" Judi asked, excitement in her voice.

Nathan reached for her hand. "The offer came last weekend, and I've decided to take it. I'll be handling the accounts for Kelly Enterprises—the company that donated the land for the church camp on the island. From what I understand, this company is a full-time job in and of itself. I'll also take on extra work like wills and probate for those on the island. It's the perfect job!"

"Van Edwards!" she whispered almost reverently, her eyes meeting his.

Nathan had to only smile his response. Whatever or whoever Mr. Edwards was, "rescuer" could easily be added to his résumé. In time, Nathan hoped to discover the real person behind this unusual and secretive old man. Mr. Edwards also indicated that the mayor's position might be opening soon if Nathan still wanted to remain active in politics. Nathan thought this might be a conflict of interest, but Van said on an island that small, everything was a conflict of interest. He was probably right!

Laurie broke in. "You'll be moving?"

Nathan nodded, his eyes never wavering from Judi. "If Judi is willing to go back to Bay Island, I'd like to sell this house and my car. With our savings and equity, we will have enough to clear our debts and start over."

"Are you sure you want to do this?" Hope was written on every feature of Judi's face. "You love this house and living in Pennsylvania."

"Yes, but I'm rather fond of the island and your golf cart, too," he answered with a laugh. "And your little VW Beetle should fit right in once we get it back in working order." Judi jumped up and hugged him with abandonment, and he leaned close to her ear. "By the way, the church turned down your resignation. Once your original Social Security number is back in order, your job will be waiting."

Obviously speechless, Judi snuggled against his shoulder. He closed his arms around her, feeling the fragility of her body.

"Besides, when we get settled," Nathan continued in low tones, "you're going to get that college education you always wanted—the honest way."

Judi looked up. "You promise?"

"I promise!"

Jeff stepped forward and placed his hand on Judi's shoulder. "I'm sorry that we treated you poorly. I can see Nathan has made an excellent choice. Right, sis?"

Laurie grudgingly agreed and walked over to join in a group hug. Nathan could tell Judi was happily reserved, but weary and near collapse. He needed to end this inquisition.

"Anyone else have anything to say to Judi or to me?"

His mother cleared her throat. "When Laurie called us this afternoon"—Nathan shot his sister a disapproving look, and she innocently shrugged—"I thought it might be good," continued his mother, unwrapping her white lacy handkerchief, "for me to give this back to Judi." A red ruby stone brooch lay in stark contrast against the white cloth.

Judi let go of Nathan and leaned forward, pale and uncertain, looking questioningly back at his mother. "It's my grandmother's brooch."

"You took it?" Nathan accused, unable to keep the disbelief from his voice.

His mother frowned. "Judi had shown it to me one time, and I knew it was something important to her. I saw it the day I helped you clean out her clothes and, well—I wanted something to remind me of her."

Like having the air sucked out of his lungs, Nathan felt sucker punched and at a loss for words. He knew the excuse was an outright lie and another example of his family's impertinence toward his wife. It was time to stand his ground.

Suddenly, Judi placed her hand on his arm and stepped forward.

"That was awfully sweet of you," Judi told his mother, taking the offered ruby. "Thank you for taking such good care of it."

His mother smiled contritely. "I should have told Nathan, but you know—"

"It's okay," Judi assured, smiling at the older woman.

Nathan was pleased to see his mother had the decency to blush. Served her right—she should be ashamed. His father remained silent throughout the exchange, but Judi didn't seem to notice.

"You're all invited," Nathan announced, breaking the intense moment as he pulled Judi to his side, "to Bay Island for a visit, especially for the ceremony to recommit our vows as we begin our lives together again. I believe our good friends, Tilly Storm and Van Edwards, have something cooked up that should prove to be a very classy celebration. You won't want to miss it."

Nathan smiled down at Judi and kissed her full on the lips. "Are you game?"

"I wouldn't miss it for the world, Mr. Whithorne!"

epilogue

Judi walked proudly down the aisle, her father's arm hooked inside hers, feeling like a redeemed Cinderella. Her simple, sea-foam chiffon dress felt light and airy, ready to sing like her heart. At the altar, Nathan looked undeniably handsome in his dashing gray suit. He sent her a quirky smile that sent waves of joy through her.

Nathan's entire family was present, attempting in their own way to mend fences. Funny how much easier it was to forgive when so much had been forgiven of her. Even her father looked attractive and clean-cut, and healthier than he'd been in years. She never thought happiness would be hers to embrace again, but here she was, sailing like a bird above crystal blue waters.

Nathan and she were stronger and better than before. Tilly and Van were insistent about planning and paying for the ceremony. Someone had to throw a party, Tilly had said.

The service was simple, but an absolute ball. Family and friends gathered at the church reception hall bubbling over with food and laughter. Judi tapped her foot to the lively brass quartet, watching Jason and Lauren sway to the music. Larry and Becky were having a great time, too, and Judi reveled in the happiness of the expecting couples. As she looked over the gathering, she realized new life was everywhere on the island.

Judi caught a glimpse of Tilly slipping through the crowd and into the kitchen. With a smile, she detached herself from the festivities to follow.

"Hey, where you going?" Nathan laughingly stole up beside her, taking her hand in his.

"To the kitchen!" Judi gave him a full smile. "I want to thank Tilly for all her hard work, including putting this together. I'm having the time of my life."

"We'll go together," he whispered in her ear.

They made their way toward the partially closed kitchen door and skidded to a stop. Judi put her hand over her mouth to keep from bursting out.

Nathan gave her a mischievous grin and immediately pulled her away into the deserted hallway. "You always said Mr. Edwards and Tilly were sweet on each other."

"But kissing in the church kitchen?" Judi laughed.

"How about in the church hallway?" Nathan asked, gently pulling her to him, his lips meeting hers. "Are you happy, Mrs. Whithorne?"

"Indubitably!"

"That's a pretty fancy word."

"I have a pretty fancy husband."

He kissed her again. "And a pretty awesome God!"

A Letter To Our Readers

Dear Reader:

In order that we might better contribute to your reading enjoyment, we would appreciate your taking a few minutes to respond to the following questions. We welcome your comments and read each form and letter we receive. When completed, please return to the following:

Fiction Editor
Heartsong Presents
P.O. Box 719
Uhrichsville, Ohio 44683

1. Did you enjoy reading *Bay Hideaway* by Beth Loughner?
   ❏ Very much! I would like to see more books by this author!
   ❏ Moderately. I would have enjoyed it more if

   _____

   _____

   _____

2. Are you a member of **Heartsong Presents**? ❏ Yes ❏ No
   If no, where did you purchase this book? _____

   _____

3. How would you rate, on a scale from 1 (poor) to 5 (superior), the cover design? _____

4. On a scale from 1 (poor) to 10 (superior), please rate the following elements.

   ____ Heroine   ____ Plot
   ____ Hero   ____ Inspirational theme
   ____ Setting   ____ Secondary characters

5. These characters were special because? _____

_____

_____

6. How has this book inspired your life? _____

_____

_____

7. What settings would you like to see covered in future
   Heartsong Presents books? _____

_____

_____

8. What are some inspirational themes you would like to see
   treated in future books? _____

_____

_____

9. Would you be interested in reading other **Heartsong
   Presents** titles? ❏ Yes ❏ No

10. Please check your age range:
    ❏ Under 18   ❏ 18-24
    ❏ 25-34   ❏ 35-45
    ❏ 46-55   ❏ Over 55

Name _____

Occupation _____

Address _____

City, State, Zip_____

Heart♥ng

Any 12 Heartsong Presents titles for only $27.00*

CONTEMPORARY ROMANCE IS CHEAPER BY THE DOZEN!

Buy any assortment of twelve *Heartsong Presents* titles and save 25% off the already discounted price of $2.97 each!

*plus $2.00 shipping and handling per order and sales tax where applicable.

HEARTSONG PRESENTS TITLES AVAILABLE NOW:

(If ordering from this page, please remember to include it with the order form.)

Presents

Great Inspirational Romance at a Great Price!

Heartsong Presents books are inspirational romances in contemporary and historical settings, designed to give you an enjoyable, spirit-lifting reading experience. You can choose wonderfully written titles from some of today's best authors like Andrea Boeshaar, Wanda E. Brunstetter, Yvonne Lehman, Joyce Livingston, and many others.

When ordering quantities less than twelve, above titles are $2.97 each.
Not all titles may be available at time of order.